J
AVI

24x8/19

P9-ECN-181

The
FIGHTING
GROUND

For Kevin and Shaun,
my sons, with love

The Fighting Ground
Copyright © 1984 by Avi. Frontispiece copyright © 1984 by Ellen Thompson.
All rights reserved. No part of this book may be used or reproduced in any manner
whatsoever without written permission except in the case of brief quotations embodied
in critical articles and reviews. Printed in the United States of America. For information
address HarperCollins Children's Books, a division of HarperCollins Publishers,
10 East 53rd Street, New York, NY 10022.
Designed by Joyce Hopkins
Frontispiece by Ellen Thompson

Library of Congress Cataloging-in-Publication Data
Avi, date
    The fighting ground.
    Summary: Thirteen-year-old Jonathan goes off to fight in the Revolutionary
War and discovers the real war is being fought within himself.
    1. United States—History—Revolution, 1775–1783—Juvenile fiction.
[1. United States—History—Revolution, 1775–1783—Fiction]
I. Title.
PZ7.A953Fi 1984   [Fic]   82-47719
ISBN 0-397-32073-6
ISBN 0-397-32074-4 (lib. bdg.)

20 19 18 17 16 15 14 13

The
FIGHTING
GROUND
by Avi

HarperCollinsPublishers

9:58

It was in the morning when Jonathan first heard the bell. He was standing in the warm, open field feeling hot, dirty, and bored. His father, not far off, limped as he worked along the newly turned rows of corn. As for Jonathan, he was daydreaming, daydreaming about being a soldier.

His older brother was a soldier with General Washington in Pennsylvania. His cousin had joined a county regiment. Jonathan kept waiting for his father to say that he too could join. He was, after all, thirteen. But his father only put him off.

Jonathan dreamed of one day taking up a gun

himself and fighting the enemy. For he had heard his father and his father's friends talk many times about the tyrannical British; their cruel mercenary allies, the German-speaking Hessians; and the hated Tories, those American traitors who had sided with the brutal English king.

But Jonathan's father no longer spoke of war. During the past winter he had fought near Philadelphia and been wounded in the leg. It was painful for him to walk, and Jonathan was needed at home. Though Jonathan kept asking questions about the battle, his father only shook his head, while his eyes grew clouded. Still, Jonathan could dream. So it was that at the sound of the bell they both stood still and listened.

The bell, at the tavern a mile and a half away, was used to call the men to arms. This time it tolled only once. Puzzled, they stood alert, straining to hear if more would come.

Jonathan looked over at the edge of the field, where his father's flintlock musket leaned against a stump. The cartridge box and powder horn were also there. The gun was primed, ready to be used. Jonathan knew how. Hadn't his father taught him, drilled him, told him that *everyone* had to be prepared? Hadn't he said, "We must all be soldiers now"? And hadn't Jonathan talked with his friends of war, battles old and new, strategies fit for major generals? And, having fought their wars, they had *always* won their glory, hadn't they?

So when the bell stayed silent, Jonathan sighed with disappointment. His father turned back to work. The beating of his hoe against the earth made a soft, yielding sound, as if a clock had begun to count a familiar piece of time.

But as Jonathan resumed his tasks, his mind turned to uniforms, the new New Jersey uniforms. He pictured himself in a fancy blue jacket with red facings, white leggings, a beautiful new gun snug against his cheek. . . .

Softly at first, but with growing sureness, the bell began to ring again. Each stoke sliced away a piece of calm.

"What do you think?" Jonathan asked.

His father pulled off his black felt hat and mopped his brow with the back of his hand. He was looking south, worry on his face. Absentmindedly, he rubbed his wounded leg.

Seeing him yet undecided, Jonathan walked to the edge of the field to get a drink of water from the clay jar by the gun. The cool water dripped down his neck, trickled over his chest, and made him shiver.

The bell tolled on. Jonathan, stealing glances at his father, touched his fingers to the glossy butt of the gun, liking its burly satin finish.

"Maybe you'd best get back to the house," his father said. "Could be someone's come on through with news. I'd need to know."

Jonathan sprang up. Too fast.

"Jonathan!" his father cried. Grabbed by his father's voice, Jonathan stood where he was.

"Don't you—by God—don't you go beyond!"

They looked at one another. Jonathan felt his stomach turn all queer, for in that moment his father's eyes became unveiled, and they revealed themselves to be full of fear.

Quickly, Jonathan turned away and began to run through the copse of trees that separated the field from their house. Behind him, the clocklike sound of his father's work resumed, an echo to the call of the bell.

10:15

Jonathan vaulted the split-rail fence, hardly breaking stride. As he came up to the house he'd lived in most of his life, his mother appeared at the door. From behind her skirts his young brother and sister poked their heads.

"What is it?" his mother called before he spoke a word. He could see her worry. Each stroke of the distant bell seemed to make her wince. She had always hated the war, even talk of war, fretting so about his brother, who had gone off and yet never sent a word, not one.

At her question Jonathan stopped short, not wanting to get too close. His bare toes curled into the soft earth. "Don't know," he replied. "Pa told me to see if anyone came through with news."

"Not here," she said.

"Maybe they're going to take back Trenton," he said. Two years before, only twenty miles away, General Washington had beaten the Hessians there. "Think they might?" he asked, looking about for his shoes. She didn't reply.

And then, as suddenly as it had begun, the ringing

7

of the bell stopped, leaving an empty silence. Jonathan wondered if he was already too late.

"Want me to go to the tavern to find out what it was?" he asked, edging closer in. He had spied his shoes. They were on the bench by the door.

"Your father tell you to?"

When Jonathan gave no reply, she pushed a slip of hair beneath her cap and slapped away a tugging child's hand. "Maybe you'd best," she said. "Your father can't. And we don't want to be surprised."

Not wanting to give her time to change her mind, Jonathan leaped forward, pulled on his shoes, then bolted up and began to run.

"Just find out!" she called after him. "Then come on right back! You hear?"

Pretending he had not heard, Jonathan kept up his steady run.

10:25

Jonathan lengthened his stride, turned a sharp angle, then beat his way to the creek. He passed the cooling house. He sped along the path that edged the old dark woods where the warm, soft smell of rotting wood filled the air.

Maybe, he thought as he ran, maybe it was going to be a battle, a big one. Maybe he would take a part.

O Lord, he said to himself, make it be a battle. With armies, big ones, and cannons and flags and drums and dress parades! Oh, he could, *would* fight. Good as his older brother. Maybe good as his pa. Better, maybe. O Lord, he said to himself, make it something *grand*!

He was running harder now, having broken from the path to the Alexandria Road. He passed the place where a boy he knew used to live; they hadn't quite been friends. He'd gone off and gotten killed. Jonathan didn't like to think of that. Besides, the boy's folks said it was an awful war, cursed it, spat on it when they could. People, hearing them, hinted they might be secret Tories. There were lots of Tories like that around, spies and turncoats all. Such folks were warned to keep their thoughts to themselves. Tories got what they deserved.

Jonathan moved up a small hill and, once on top, paused to catch his breath. A swirl of red-breasted pigeons coursed the air. A squirrel scolded, a crow

9

cackled. It was spring, and warm, and wonderful ripe for war. Jonathan felt sure he could try anything, be anything, do anything anyone might set before him.

And even as he stood there, unsure what to do, the bell resumed its vibrant call. He could go home . . . or to the tavern.

But if he went to the tavern, he knew it wouldn't be just to get the news. He meant to go and fight.

"Do it!" he told himself. *"Go and fight!"* His father was afraid, but he wasn't. And again he began to pelt toward the sound of the bell, his blood as warm as the swollen, spring-tied earth.

10:45

The tavern was the biggest place around, and was perched on the highest point. Built entirely of stone, it seemed a fortress, a castle at the crossroads, with sparkling glass windows and a high, peaked roof.

To the south seven miles was Pennington. Twenty miles distant was Trenton town. The British and the hated Hessians held them both.

Ten miles to the northwest lay Alexandria. Fleming was six miles north by east, and to the west, hugging the big river, lay Well's Ferry. Americans held those towns. Jonathan had been to none of them, American or British held.

As he approached the tavern, Jonathan could see the bell. A friend, a boy his own age, was heaving the cord. The bell hung in its own rack, set up to sound alarms. It stood to one side of the green where the men practiced for militia duty, an exercise that Jonathan dearly loved to watch.

Some men had already gathered at the tavern and were busy talking. Becoming shy, Jonathan slowed his pace. As he approached, a man climbed a tree to watch the roads.

Jonathan wished someone would tell him what was happening. But no one paid him mind. He thought: They don't know I've come to fight.

"Here comes someone!" cried the man in the tree.

"Got his gun?"

"Looks it!"

Cartridge pouches, powder horns, and guns had been left against the tavern. Jonathan wished he'd brought his father's gun.

He felt a tap on his shoulder. "Your father coming?" was the question.

Before he could reply, someone else said: "His leg's still sitting poor."

They paid no more mind to Jonathan.

Frustrated, he went over to the bell. Though he would rather have spoken to the men, he talked to his young friend. "What's going?" he asked.

"Soldiers," said his friend, fitting the word between strokes of the bell.

A whip of excitement cut through Jonathan.

"Enemy ones?" he asked.

"That's what they say," his friend replied.

11:00

As Jonathan watched, a man came out of the tavern, someone he had never seen before. He was a large man, with broad shoulders and a red, badly pockmarked face. His shirt, spilling out of his trousers, wasn't very clean, and his dark-green jacket with fraying cuffs was clearly old. His boots were caked with mud, his hat was too small.

When the man came out of the tavern, he was

holding a tankard with one hand, wiping crumbs from his mouth with the other. He stood in front of the tavern door, surveying the gathered men who, in turn, kept keen eyes on him.

"Any more coming?" the stranger called.

"Be some time yet" came the reply.

"We don't have time," the stranger snapped. He took a half step around as if to go back inside. The tavern keeper stood in the doorway.

"By God," the stranger said, "don't they understand? If we don't move, they'll get through."

The tavern keeper said nothing at all.

A man came running, cresting the hill. A gun was in his hand. "Where they coming from?" he called.

"Pennington way," called one of the men.

"How many?"

"Fifteen or less."

"Who saw them?"

"The Corporal's come."

Again, heads turned to the stranger. He was finishing off his drink. When done, he handed the tankard to the keeper, who took it silently.

"Here's more!" cried the man in the tree. "You be patient, Corporal," he called to the stranger. "You'll have an army yet."

The tavern keeper shook his head. "It's ground-breaking time."

The Corporal strode down from the doorway and approached the men.

"How long will it take marching troops to get here from Linvale?" he asked.

"That's four miles" came an answer.

"An hour and a half" was the calculation.

Impatiently, the stranger rubbed his hands together, then suddenly swung around to face the bell, where Jonathan was standing, watching.

"That's enough!" the Corporal barked to Jonathan's friend. "They'll either come or not."

The boy let the rope drop.

Again the stranger considered the group of men, then, turning, discovered Jonathan's eyes fixed on him.

"You handle a gun?" he asked.

"Yes, sir," Jonathan managed to get out.

"And you?" the stranger asked the other boy. The boy shook his head no.

The Corporal glowered, then shifted around once more and drifted toward the men. Four more had run in, making thirteen in all. The Corporal appraised them, then turned to the tavern keeper. "You coming?" he asked.

"We'll need to have ourselves a second line in case they get through," said the innkeeper. "I'd best stick here."

The Corporal frowned and then, lost in thought, went to his horse and tightened up the saddle.

Only then did it occur to Jonathan that this Corporal, whoever he was, had ridden in with the news. He wondered where he had come from and just what he had seen, and why he'd come to this place.

When he finished fussing with his horse, the Corporal swung around to face the waiting men. "There's no more time," he said. "We need to go."

Jonathan noticed that the men were now watching one another as much as they watched the stranger.

"Aren't we going to wait for more?" came the question.

"It's late," the Corporal replied. "Yes or no? Are we going?"

No one spoke. Then someone, Jonathan didn't see who, gave a murmur. Others took it up, a brief swelling sound, not quite a word.

"All right," the Corporal said, choosing to take the sound as "yes." He looked about again, his eyes coming to rest on Jonathan.

"You," he said, pointing. "You said you could shoot. Get a musket from the tavern. You're needed."

11:30

His pride soaring, Jonathan grinned at his friend, who was looking at him with astonishment. Then Jonathan turned toward the tavern keeper, who was standing by the door.

"Going, are you?" the tavern keeper said before Jonathan could speak.

"Yes, sir."

"Got asked special, did you?"

Jonathan nodded yes.

"What's your father to say?"

"Told me to come."

"Did he?"

Jonathan didn't say.

"And now," said the tavern keeper, "our blessed Corporal asks to borrow a gun."

"I can use it."

"Hope you can," said the tavern keeper. He moved inside, saying, "Come on."

Jonathan bounded up the steps. It was dark inside. The wooden floorboards, shiny from heavy use, glowed with a dark-brown warmth. The rank smell of ale and cider thickened the air.

Waiting just inside the door, Jonathan kept his

eyes on the far end of the large, dim room, where the white glow of the keeper's shirt moved behind the grill.

Within moments the man emerged from the dark, a gun in his hand. It was a flintlock musket, almost six feet long, butt and stock of polished wood. Jonathan saw that it was older than his father's gun, but to him it was nothing less than beautiful.

Reaching out with one hand, he put his fingers around the cold metal barrel. It was unexpectedly heavy. He had to thrust out his other hand to keep it up.

Holding it tightly, he brought the gun close to his chest, then let it swing down till the butt rested on the floor. The gun reached above his head.

"Manage?" the tavern keeper asked.

"Yes, sir," said Jonathan. "Sure. I can—"

"It's twelve pounds of weight."

Jonathan studied the gun, from its topmost ramrod to its shiny hammer lock to its bottom butt plate. Knowing the gun was his to use, he felt a deep glow inside.

"Have I got your word of honor you'll bring it back?"

"Yes, sir."

"Your honor as a man?"

"Yes, sir."

The tavern keeper strung a cartridge pouch around the boy's neck. "Thirty cartridges," he said. "Wrapped them myself. Here's your powder." He added the powder horn.

"Any extra flint?" Jonathan asked, wanting to show he understood what he was about.

"What I've got to spare is on the gun." The tavern keeper kept studying Jonathan, measuring him. "Look here," he finally said, "you don't have to go. You can leave all this and get on out through the back. No one's going to know, or care. Not that man. Just because he's tapped you doesn't mean you have to go. He likes telling folks what to do."

Jonathan, not even wanting to hear the words, looked down. He fingered the gun nervously.

"You know much about him?" the tavern keeper asked.

Jonathan shook his head no.

The tavern keeper considered. Then he sighed. "You take care of yourself," he said.

For a moment Jonathan remained standing there, not knowing what to say.

"Get on then, if you're going," the man said with a wave of his hand. "Get!"

Jonathan turned, inadvertently smashing the gun butt against the doorframe. The shock made him almost drop the gun. Recovering, he hastened outside into the light.

The men had already begun to move south along the Pennington Road. The Corporal, astride his horse, was rounding past the bend. Jonathan looked about. Behind him, from the building's darkness, the tavern keeper watched, while in front his friend sat on the bell-rack frame, hands to either side. He too was watching.

Grasping the gun tightly in both hands, Jonathan jumped down the steps and ran down the road toward Pennington.

12:05

The gun was heavy. Jonathan tried throwing it over his shoulder and resting it as the others did, only to find its weight cut into his neck. He had to use both hands and carry it across his chest. He didn't like the notion that he was the only one who held his gun that way. Still, he had no choice. There were the cartridge box and powder horn, too. They kept thumping against his legs, the straps having been cut for a tall man.

When they clattered over the first wooden bridge south of the crossroads, Jonathan was still far behind. A little farther on came another bridge. He saw the Corporal had called a stop before they crossed it, and from his horse he was talking to the men. Hurrying, Jonathan ran to catch up, but missed the first part of what had been said.

". . . at least that's my figuring," he heard the Corporal say. "It couldn't be helped. But we can stop them if we've stomach enough. They won't think we'll try."

"How many do you think they'll be?" called a man.

Jonathan, on the outer fringe of the group, strained to listen, glad to be able to rest his gun on the ground.

"Twenty, twenty-five" came the Corporal's off-handed reply.

His words were met with uneasy silence. Jonathan, sensing that something was wrong, looked around.

"Before, you said that they weren't more than fifteen" came an angry voice.

"Did I?" said the Corporal coolly. "Then I misspoke myself."

Again, save for the shifting feet of the men, there was a silence. Jonathan noticed how nervous they were. It hadn't occurred to him that they would be.

"Does five more turn you about?" the Corporal asked.

Jonathan looked from face to face, waiting for a reply. He saw downcast eyes, furtive and unsure.

Then someone said, "I want to hear again what brought them out. You said a Committee of Public Safety. Aside from yourself, how many were there?"

The Corporal's face turned redder. "Ask them," he snapped.

"Here," came a tense voice, "*we* didn't elect you Corporal. Sitting on a horse don't make you so damn high."

"You can choose for yourself" came the return, and angrily the Corporal swung down from his horse. "I just beg you gentlemen to make it fast. While you're holding your congress, they're coming closer. Who will ye have?"

Jonathan watched the shifting eyes. No one said a word. No one looked directly at the Corporal.

"Then, by God," the Corporal snapped, "I'll be your man. Is that your silent meaning?"

Jonathan, trying to understand what was happening, saw the men shift about. No one spoke a word. They seemed cowed.

Quickly, the Corporal remounted. "Come on, then," he said. "We need to get to Rocktown before they do. We can ambush them from the trees if that's your pleasure."

The notion of an ambush rather than an open fight cheered the men. Jonathan saw the tension ease. A few men grinned.

Turning his horse, the Corporal moved on toward the bridge. The men followed briskly.

Jonathan gathered up his gun and hurried after. For himself, he was glad the Corporal led them. He thought him a strong, forceful man.

12:30

When they crossed over the second bridge, the road began to rise. The pace slowed. Some of the men were breathing hard. Jonathan, with a sudden burst, caught up.

For a while he walked along with a man he knew to be his father's friend. A large man, he was already perspiring. His bald head was bright and wet. A fringe of whitened hair dripped sweat.

"What's it about?" asked Jonathan, taking a step and a half to match each of the strides of the bigger man.

The man gave Jonathan a quick look as if surprised to see him there. Instead of giving an answer, he said, "What are you doing here?"

"Going to fight," said Jonathan. "I heard there were enemy troops. Fifteen, twenty or so. Where are they going? What are they trying to do? Something happen?"

The man studied Jonathan, then turned and spat on the ground. "Didn't you hear?" he asked.

"Just what I said."

The man sucked a deep breath and marched in heavy silence. Waiting for an answer, Jonathan did his best to keep up. Suddenly, the man said, "Why'd you come?"

"What?"

"Why'd you come, I asked you."

Jonathan searched for words. "Wanted to," he said.

"Your father know? Give permission?"

"Yes, sir," said Jonathan, half swallowing his words.

"How's his leg?"

"Still poor."

"Maybe he's better off," said the man. Then he said, "You sure he sent you?"

Jonathan, feeling uncomfortable, let the man move on ahead. The man didn't look back but continued to march on.

Once more Jonathan allowed himself to drop to the rear, deciding it was better to stay last. As he started to march again, however, he realized his father's friend hadn't replied to his questions. The thought came to him: Perhaps he didn't have the answers.

12:40

When the road reached the top of a ridge, they paused once more. It was hotter, much more humid. Jonathan scanned the sky, noticing clouds building to the west.

Even though they hadn't gone long, some of the men threw themselves on the ground as if exhausted. Others sprawled against trees. Most removed their hats. Some fanned themselves. The

Corporal alone seemed anxious to get on. Atop his horse, he kept his eyes on the road ahead.

Jonathan rested by a tree. His legs weren't tired, but his arms ached. He placed his gun against the tree and studied where they were.

Off to one side of the ridge he could see a small, meandering creek and two small ponds that fed it. Thick woods stood beyond the pond. Farther on, perhaps half a mile, were more high hills. To the south it was also high and heavily wooded. Jonathan could see where the road ran south and climbed again. At the highest point, only a little way beyond, was Rocktown, where they were going to fight.

He looked back and took measure of the clouds. A storm was coming, a big one. He gazed about again. It was so quiet. He could hear no birds. Not even the men were talking. Nor was there any wind, not the smallest hint of a breeze. The leaves on the trees, spring new and kelly green, hung limp. Such birds as there were flew too high.

The stillness made him uneasy. It was as if nothing was allowed to move but themselves, rushing on—to what, he was not sure.

Suddenly aware that his heart was beating fast, he felt a great need to know what was happening and what he had to do. But he was afraid of the kinds of questions his father's friend had asked. He didn't want to be noticed too much. They might send him home. Reluctantly, he decided he would just have to wait, and learn by watching the others.

12:50

"Corporal!" someone called. "Where's your Snydertown folks?"

Jonathan had heard of Snydertown. He believed it was three miles somewhere to the east, but wasn't sure. He was already farther from his home than he'd been in many months.

"They joining us?" someone else threw in.

Jonathan could see from the way the men were watching that these were important questions.

"Wouldn't be fair for us to do their work," added another.

The Corporal shifted slowly and gazed stony faced down the road. Some of the men looked knowingly at one another.

"We going or not?" asked the Corporal. He spoke without looking back.

"You've got a reputation for being overfond of killing," someone said. "That ever reach your ears?"

That time the Corporal turned. "Sir," he said evenly, "if they do come, it'll be your home they'll burn, as well as mine."

No more words were spoken. Instead, slowly, the men came to their feet. The Corporal urged his horse forward. Silently, the men followed.

So did Jonathan. But he saw that once again the men had grown uneasy. In the face of the man who had last spoken, he thought he recognized the same look his father had had when they parted: fear.

1:00

Marching made Jonathan feel better. He started to whistle. But someone in front swiveled around and gave him an angry look. Jonathan stopped whistling. The silence pressed him once again.

1:05

After a slight dip the road began to rise. The men moved slower. It wasn't long before Jonathan was marching in their midst. He wished they would talk, but words came very seldom.

"Your wife," he heard one man ask another. "She is perhaps better?"

Jonathan recognized the man. He was one of the French people who had lately come to live in the area. He spoke with an accent.

"She's better" came the reply.

"That is very good," the Frenchman said. The conversation ended.

The only sound was the shuffling of feet, an empty and hollow sound. Jonathan wondered how many such hollow steps it would take for them to reach the fighting ground.

1:30

Clustered about a water well, Rocktown consisted of six houses by the road. Jonathan couldn't recall if he'd been there before. It looked familiar. But then, most of the houses thereabouts looked very much the same.

He puzzled over the name "Rocktown." He saw no rocks. He wondered if there was a nearby quarry. He thought his father had gone there a few months ago. He tried to remember why, but couldn't. It annoyed him that he couldn't.

The men stopped at the well, where a woman was drawing water. She didn't pause in her work, nor did she speak. But the band of men clearly made her uneasy.

Jonathan watched her with curiosity, trying to guess her thoughts. How could she just be doing nothing when so much was about to happen?

"Let's be quick about it," the Corporal called. He had—as before—remained seated on his horse.

The woman grew agitated under the scrutiny of the men. "Here," she finally said, as she drew the water-filled bucket up. "You can have it."

It was the Frenchman who, stepping forward, touched his forehead and said, *"Merci."* Grasping the bucket in his hands, he drank deeply. Then he passed the bucket to the next. Most of the men drank. No one offered anything to Jonathan. He was too shy to ask.

The woman watched the bucket go around. "Where are you heading?" she asked.

Jonathan was surprised by her question. He had thought that everyone would know the fighting was to come.

"Enemy troops are headed this way," the Corporal said.

"Here?" exclaimed the woman. Her face had turned pale.

"If we don't stop them."

It took a moment for the woman to absorb the news. "From which way?" she asked. Her voice was small. One hand was at her throat.

"Up from Pennington."

With a suddenness that took them all by surprise, the woman gathered up her skirts, turned, and fled. It made the men laugh. Jonathan wasn't sure why it seemed funny, but it did.

Only the Corporal hadn't laughed. "It's time to go," he said.

The laughter had eased the men. It was as if seeing the woman frightened made them feel better. I won't be scared the way she was, Jonathan thought.

As they got ready to move again, they kept watching the house into which the woman had fled.

Sure enough, she reappeared in a few moments with two young children and an old man. Hurriedly, they began swinging the wooden shutters over their windows. Then they rushed back inside. The door slammed loudly. The house looked dead.

The men laughed again. Without any warning, one of them raised his gun and fired into the air.

Everyone jumped.

The Corporal whirled, his face a crimson red. The man who had shot the gun was grinning broadly. "Damn you!" the Corporal cried. "Want them to know we're here?"

The grinning man looked about. He saw that others were also angry.

"Just a joke," he said, his grin fading.

"Fool!" the Corporal barked.

The man turned red.

"Now, damn all, hurry," said the Corporal. "We're late as it is." He kicked at his horse. Sullenly, all the laughter gone, the men went too.

For a moment Jonathan remained behind, upset. He turned to look at the Rocktown homes. From some of them people emerged. They stood watching as the band moved off. Jonathan began to find his pride again. They were, he reminded himself, looking at him, for he too was a soldier. Then, realizing he was being left behind, he bolted down the road.

2:05

Half a mile south of Rocktown the road reached its highest point. The men moved slowly, almost reluctantly, to its crest. The Corporal, impatient as ever, kept the lead. At the top he jumped to the ground.

They had arrived.

2:10

Some of the men sat down, some lay on their backs. Jonathan noticed a number had brought flasks and were taking drinks. He wished he had taken some water at the Rocktown well. He was thirsty now.

A few of the men went to where the Corporal stood. Side by side they studied the road, which sloped gradually down toward the south.

It was a wide valley through which the road passed,

as if the road itself had once been a river that now ran dry. Trees to either side rose up like palisades. Because the road turned, it wasn't possible to see very far, no more than a quarter mile.

Jonathan looked back over his shoulder. The clouds had rolled up higher. They were thunder-clouds of deep gray-blue, rising columns of layered darkness. If it rained, he knew, it would come hard, making it difficult for them to fire their guns.

The men, including the Corporal, paid no mind to the clouds. Instead, they continued looking down the road that went beyond the hill.

'We'll wait for them here," the Corporal said.

"They'll have to come on up," agreed one man. "Rising men shoot high," he added.

They all considered that.

"Thought you said we'd ambush them!" It was the man Jonathan had tried to talk to, his father's friend. His face was pale, tense.

"We could, sure we could," agreed another quickly. "It'd be better. It would."

The Corporal shook his head. "No place to hide behind," he replied. "Too wide. No walls. No fences. Nothing."

"Trees," suggested someone.

"We have any rifles here?" the Corporal asked,

looking about. "No. Just smooth bore. We'd be too far away." He turned about and acknowledged the storm clouds. "And if a wind comes up, it'll blow our shot to nothing. We'll line up here," he said firmly.

Jonathan's father's friend objected, shaking his head violently. "No," he said, "I don't care for it." He glanced about, seeking support from others. "We drill. We do. Regular. But not against such as these." He made a nod of his head as if to suggest what was coming up the road.

His words brought a nervous quiet. Then someone said, "I'm willing to stand here. I can't see any other way." It was the man who had shot off his gun in Rocktown.

The Corporal took off his hat and pushed back his hair. "All agreed?" he asked.

No one replied.

"How much longer you think they'll be?" someone asked.

"Soon enough."

"Where's your Snydertown folks, Corporal? That's what I'd like to know," someone called from the side of the road.

The Corporal kept his eyes down the road.

"They better come," said another. "You and them, you all started this."

The Corporal's mouth pinched tighter.

It was then that Jonathan first heard the distant tapping of the drum. As the others caught the sound, they lifted their heads. Steadily, monotonously, the tapping came. To it was added the high, piercing squeal of a fife. It slit through the air like the cutting edge of a blade.

Slowly, the men on the ground stood up.

"They be coming," someone said.

2:30

Nobody moved. They just stood there, listening to the drum. It came loud and regular, like an angry clock. Then slyly, the fife music slid into a playful tune, poking, plucking at their brittle senses. A tightness ran up and down Jonathan's spine, into the nape of his neck. He tried to cough, only to realize he had been holding his breath.

He looked about. The men were all staring. What they were seeing he couldn't tell. One man pressed an open hand to his jaw, drawing his fingers across, pulling at his lips, making them grotesque. Another man kept licking his lips.

The Corporal listened with great intensity, as if the sound of fife and drum brought a special message to his ears.

"Line! Line!" he suddenly shouted, springing to life. "Line here! Seven in front! The short ones! The rest in back! The taller. Damn all, gentlemen, hurry!"

The men began to run forward and back in a frenzy. Jonathan, not understanding where he should stand, stood in place where he was until he felt a hard slap against his back.

"Move!" came the angry command.

Mechanically, he turned toward the Corporal who, reaching out, took hold of his shoulder and shoved him forward, then spun him into position. "Front line!" he ordered. "Front line!"

Jonathan stayed where he had been put.

But other men came forward. There was more pushing, more shoving. The Corporal, holding to his horse's bridle, tried to keep the beast calm, all the while shouting directions.

"Here, here! No, fool, there! Take your place! Damn all, there! No, there. Two paces back! Dress your lines! Not right behind! Dress them, you fools! Gentlemen, your lines!"

Jonathan found himself moved this way and that, one step this direction, two the other. People stepped on his feet. The Corporal attempted to mount his horse, only to slip and fall to the ground. The men gawked, but made no move to help. The Corporal sprang up on his own. This time he climbed up successfully. Holding a pistol in one hand, he wheeled his horse about in a useless circle.

Jonathan could hear the breathing of the men all about, quick and agitated. Beyond that, he heard the tap-tapping of the drum, the nagging, relentless curl of the fife.

"There!" cried the Corporal. "That's it. Now, gentlemen, load your guns, for God's sake. Load your guns!"

All around came thudding as guns dropped to the ground, stocks to earth, followed by the pop of snaps, as leather cartridge pouches opened.

"You, boy!" came a cry. "Do your loading! Are you daft! Load your gun!"

2:35

Hurriedly, Jonathan lowered his gun to the ground. With one hand he held the muzzle, with the other he tried to open the cartridge pouch. The fastening would not give. He placed the gun on the ground before his feet.

"Pick that up, you idiot!" came a shout into his ear.

In a panic, Jonathan reached down and snatched up his gun. Resting it in the crook of his arm and clumsily using both hands, he yanked his cartridge pouch open. The wooden catch broke. His fingers, trembling, touched the cartridges. He pulled one up. It was made of rough, brown paper twisted into a tube, one end further twisted tight like a candle wick. The small package contained a measure of gunpowder and one lead ball.

Putting the twisted paper to his mouth, Jonathan tore at it with his teeth. It did not give. He tugged harder. This time the paper tore—too much. He could taste powder on his tongue. He spat it out.

Hands shaking, he tried to maneuver the gun upright while still holding the torn cartridge so it wouldn't spill. But the barrel was too high. He had to stand on his toes to pour the powder in. Then, crumpling the paper in his fist, he wadded it around the lead ball, poking both into the barrel mouth.

Unsteadily, Jonathan yanked out the ramrod from beneath the gun barrel, where it was lodged. He reached high, higher, trying to stick the swinging rod into the barrel so as to set the ball snug proper. Just managing to get the rod in, he waited for it to slide down. It would not drop. He had to reach high again, stretching on his toes as far as he could, pushing on the rod and pressing it against the wadded ball but not pressing too hard, lest he crush the powder grains and make the gun misfire.

Jonathan pulled out the rod and let it drop to the ground, only to remember that that was wrong. He bent over to pick it up, pointing the gun barrel down. To his horror the lead ball rolled out of the gun mouth onto the ground. Frantic, he snatched it up, hoping no one had seen what had happened. He flipped the ball back down into the gun.

Again he bent over, this time making sure the gun kept pointing up. The ball stayed in. Grabbing the rod, he shoved it into the muzzle once more, pressing the load tightly. Then he pulled the rod out and placed it correctly in its socket.

Holding the loaded gun before him, pointing it

waveringly forward and up, he reached for his pow-der horn and brought it around. With his teeth, he edged off the cap. Trying not to put in too much or too little, he trickled fine firing grains into the priming pan beneath the hammer lock and flint.

That done, he pushed the cap back on the horn and let it drop. Then he brought the gun upright with both hands.

He was ready at last.

2:40

Sweating all over, hoping no one had seen his clumsy slowness, Jonathan glanced about. No one was looking at him. Guns ready, faces rigid, the men were staring down the road. Even as he watched, Jonathan saw one of the men stick out his tongue, lick his lips, then hastily wipe away the spittle. Another man kept clearing his throat. A third rubbed an irritated eye.

Only then did Jonathan realize how much closer was the sound of fife and drum. He snapped his head about. At the end of the road, as it came out from behind the tall trees, soldiers were advancing.

2:41

Jonathan watched, spellbound, as the troops marched into view. Three by three they came, ten rows, thirty soldiers, all moving in lockstep, their legs lifting high and stiff.

Though still at the bottom of the hill, the soldiers seemed enormous. Never had he seen such men. Giants.

In the growing gloom of the darkening clouds their golden, pointed caps glowed brightly. Many wore great mustaches. Their jackets were blue with red cuffs and bright white buttons, their vests dark yellow. Their trousers, striped in red and white, met boots of crow-feather black. Each had a bayonet at his waist, a crossed white sash around his chest. And in his left hand each carried a tall flintlock gun.

"Hessians," the man next to Jonathan said. *"Hessians."* The words filled the air with a dreadful weight.

2:43

Jonathan felt the men around him shift uneasily, sensing the fear that had settled over the group like a suffocating blanket.

Hessians. The butchers of Long Island . . .

"So many of them . . ." came a strained voice from right behind.

Hessians. The mercenaries who killed for coin . . .

"Shut up!" roared the Corporal, trying to keep his voice under control. "No talking. Stand your ground!"

"Them's grenadiers," came another voice, unnaturally high. "See how big they are? Their match cases? See them? Do you see that boys? Grenadiers."

As Jonathan watched, the enemy troops continued to pace themselves to the beat of the drum. He couldn't see the drummer or the player, but he knew they must be boys. Perhaps, he thought, they were younger than he. He wanted to see them, wanted them to be much younger.

The Hessians continued to march.

"Keep your lines!" the Corporal shouted. "Keep them!"

The men lifted their guns and pointed them straight down the road at the oncoming soldiers.

"Hold your fire till I tell you!" the Corporal shouted. "Don't waste your shot. They're still too far!"

Jonathan could not take his eyes from the advancing troops. All of them had cleared the bend now, moving so steadily that Jonathan wondered if they saw that the road was blocked. But just as he had the thought, they came to a stop, and the smooth flow of their march broke with a clumsiness that momentarily eased Jonathan's tension.

On his horse, the Hessian officer cantered forward, looking up the hill at the Americans.

Jonathan hefted his gun a little higher. He glanced behind. His father's friend, his head glistening with sweat, was there.

"Aim low!" the Corporal cried. "Or your shot'll go high!"

Jonathan looked at his own gun. At the moment it felt light. He stole a look at the men around him. He saw their fingers flex, grip, release, and grip again.

"Where's your goddamn Snydertown Committee, Corporal?" came a call. "Why don't they come? Is there something we don't know?"

The Corporal, never taking his eyes from the Hessians, and keeping his back to his own men, said nothing. His horse, blowing out its breath, shifted nervously.

Jonathan's mouth felt hard and dry, his tongue thick. A bad taste was in his mouth. Whom could he ask for a drink? Who wouldn't mind? He gazed about, trying to pick someone, thinking only that he was more thirsty than he had ever been in his life. But the men were all too fixed upon the road for him to ask. He did not dare to speak.

Down the road the Hessians remained standing still. Only the officer on the horse was moving. Jonathan heard the sharp clop of its hooves. The officer's large mustache was turned up at either end. He carried no gun, but there was a sword in his hand that flashed in the steel-gray light. He kept looking up the hill, craning his neck now this way, now that.

Jonathan suddenly realized that he had never seen an enemy soldier before. He had seen Tories, but hateful as they were, they were only Americans. What he was seeing right before him were real enemies, foreign ones, the most awful ones, the cruel German-speaking kind.

Down the road the Hessian officer waved his sword and shouted something to his men. The drum began to beat again. The fife played high, reedy notes. From behind Jonathan felt the wind cold against his neck. The gun, swaying, felt heavy.

"Spread out a bit," the Corporal ordered. "Don't give so much target."

Everyone shifted.

"When I give the call," he continued, "the first line fires. Then the second moves on forward. You on the first line, you step back and load again. You get that? Two rounds a minute, boys, two!"

Jonathan's heart sank. *Two rounds a minute.* He couldn't do it. He wished he'd practiced more.

The tramp of the soldiers cut through his regrets. Jonathan turned. The Hessians, their red-and-white legs moving in high-stepping, winking unison, had begun once more to advance. Their guns rose beside their golden caps.

The sight made Jonathan dizzy. He swayed. The gun felt heavier.

"You are ready?" he heard close to his ear. Jonathan turned. It was the Frenchman. He was standing next to him.

Jonathan tried to answer, but found he had no voice. He nodded.

"They are the big ones, certainly," said the Frenchman.

"Steady boys, keep steady!" the Corporal called, moving off to one side. "Remember, there's a storm coming. If it rains, keep your pans covered and dry. Wait till we've got fifty yards between us, boys, fifty yards or less, fifty yards or less!"

How far, Jonathan wondered, was fifty yards? How many feet was that? What spot would that be on the road? Would anyone tell him? Why didn't anyone tell him anything? Don't they know, he said to himself, that I'm the youngest here?

His heart beat with every stroke of the drum; the soldiers advanced to the self-same sound. If his heart stopped beating, Jonathan wondered, would they stop too?

Watching, he couldn't believe how they came together, shoulder to shoulder, no one moving out of step, their legs lifting stiffly, perfectly.

The Hessian officer shouted something.

"What did he say?" asked one of the Americans.

"Don't know."

"What's he saying?"

"Ready!" cried the Corporal.

Feeling the backs of his legs grow tight, Jonathan pulled his gun up. He tried to sight down along the muzzle, tried to remember to aim low, but was afraid to point down lest he lose the ball again. The gun lurched up, down, right and left. It took all his strength to keep it still. His back hurt. The Hessians kept coming closer. Should he aim at someone, he wondered? Who?

He heard a click. The Frenchman had drawn back his flintlock. Jonathan pulled one of his hands away from his gun to do the same. The gun dipped dangerously. He grabbed the lock anyway, yanking back. It came with a snap.

"Steady!" shouted the Corporal. "Steady!" Jonathan was sure the Corporal was shouting at him alone.

He watched the blue coats, the crossed white sashes, the tall yellow caps. They were, he thought, no more than two hundred feet away. Why are they here? he asked himself. Why are they coming toward me? He felt his skin prickle. His stomach hurt.

The Hessian officer shouted more words that Jonathan could not understand. Without warning, the Hessians began to shift, some to the right and some to the left, until as if by magic they were no longer three in a row but ten men to the line: an advancing wall.

"Almost!" cried the Corporal.

Again the Hessian officer shouted. Upon his command, the soldiers lowered their guns. Without missing a step they snapped their bayonets onto their guns, presenting the glistening blades directly at the Americans.

Jonathan tried to swallow. He could not. His throat was too stiff, too dry. He was so thirsty.

A sudden explosion burst from the American line. Someone had fired.

The Corporal screamed a curse. His horse reared. Someone else fired.

A wave of hysteria welled up inside Jonathan. His arms tensed. Without meaning to, he pulled the trigger. There was a flash and an explosion as the musket jerked against his body, spinning him halfway around.

More guns fired. Explosions burst about his ears, the percussion punching him like unseen fists.

"Out of my way!" someone screamed at him, roughly shoving him aside. Jonathan almost fell as another man pushed past him. More explosions, this time in front of him. Someone began to cry, "O Lord, O Lord."

Jonathan's ears rang. His eyes were smarting. The air was thick with smoke, and stank.

He knew that he had to reload and shoot again,

but he stood where he was, confused. Why were things happening so quickly? It was unfair. The smoke got thicker. He could not see through it to understand what was happening. On all sides guns kept shooting. Sometimes they went off two at a time. Then came long, terrible empty pauses when nothing happened at all. Then orange flashes burst through the smoke again. Through it all, Jonathan heard the Corporal's voice raging above the din: "In line! In line! In order, idiots! Damn all, in order!"

The smoke shifted, briefly lifting. The Hessians moved closer yet, their lines unbroken, their bayonets thrust forward, their drum pounding, their fife screaming.

2:50

Jonathan plunged his hand into his cartridge case, took out a cartridge, and bit through the twisted paper end. Hurriedly he went through the loading steps, trying to think only of what he had to do, concentrating so hard his head hurt.

When his gun was once more loaded, he lifted it. Drawing back the lock, he looked about, prepared to fire. But there he paused, bewildered, not sure which way to shoot. A roar of muskets came from one side, followed by another. The wind seemed to rise. Nearby came a loud, thick sound, a heavy "Huff!" as if someone had lost his breath. A weight fell against him, then tumbled to the ground. Jonathan stepped aside. His father's friend lay upon the ground, his legs twisted under him, eyes open wide, arms flung to either side, his sweaty blouse red with blood.

"In order! In order!" came the Corporal's piercing cry.

Jonathan knelt by the fallen man's side.

Another crash of gunfire came, followed by another.

Jonathan put his hand to the man's face, touching it with shaking fingers. The flesh was soft, wet, and warm.

Jonathan reached for his gun. It wasn't where he thought it was. Turning, he found it, but when he pulled at it, it wouldn't come. His eyes followed its line. The gun was caught under someone's twisting body—the Frenchman's.

Afraid to get closer, Jonathan's first thought was to leave the gun. Just as quickly, he told himself that he had to get it, that it wasn't his but borrowed, that he had to bring it back. It was his responsibility, his duty, his word.

Twisting awkwardly, the Frenchman lurched up on his hands and knees. His head, hanging low, moved from side to side. Blood dripped to the ground.

With a growing sense of horror, Jonathan took up the gun, then stood. The smoke had cleared from the road. The Hessian line was standing erect, guns high, aiming. As he watched, one of the Hessians dropped his gun and crumpled forward, his bright, golden cap hitting the ground and bouncing twice before it came to rest.

The Corporal had a musket in his hands and was reloading. His lips were drawn back from his teeth.

Jonathan searched for other Americans. They seemed to have gone. He whirled about. He saw them behind him, quickly backing away.

A shout came from the Hessian lines. Jonathan turned again. The Hessians had lowered their guns. Their bayonets were thrust forward ready to charge. As Jonathan watched, they began to trot forward, directly toward where he stood.

With a shock he realized that he was standing

alone, and that the entire line of enemy troops was rushing at him and at no one else.

He spun about and began to run.

3:01

Jonathan ran away from the road, tripping, sprawling, falling on his knees. In one motion he sprang up, using his gun as a staff, and twisted to look back. A rapid rattle of musket shots came from a completely unexpected place. He stood transfixed, feeling lost, incapable of deciding which way to go. Where had the others gone? Where was the Corporal? Why hadn't they waited? Why hadn't they taken him along?

In his confusion, Jonathan turned a half circle, only to see three Hessian soldiers charging in his direction.

"*Halt!*" came the cry.

One of the soldiers stopped, lifted his gun, and fired. Jonathan saw the plume of flame, and heard the hard report. Whirling, he ran again.

He ran in terror, straining every muscle, pumping his legs, his arms, not daring to look back. His

only salvation was the protection of the woods—
he plunged among the trees. Several times the heavy
gun almost slipped from his hands. He clutched at
it frantically, grabbing it back when it started to fall
as if it were the linchpin that held what was left of
him together.

Shouts and shots pursued him from behind,
branches and vines caught at him. His side ached
terribly. His cartridge box and powder horn kept
banging against his knees. Pulling them from around
his neck, he flung them away. His foot caught upon
a root. He crashed down, seeing nothing but a blur
of green, his breath blown, completely spent, leaving him without the strength to move at all.

3:05

He lay upon the ground telling himself that he had
to get up. Yet he could not. Exhausted, he remained
where he was. Gunshots crackled dimly in the distance. A whispering wind, carrying the echo of the
fife, floated high. Then it all grew faint and fainter
still until the only sounds were forest sounds. Soon
they too drifted from his mind, leaving only silence.

3:16

In the immense silence all that Jonathan could hear was his own breath. It came at first in short, reaching gasps. As it slowed to normal, he felt a pain growing inside, a pain spreading through his body, pressing from within.

He began to cry. The cry came at first in pieces, as if the cry itself had been shattered and existed only in fragmentary, jagged bits. But bit by bit the cry grew whole, taking over until every part of him cried.

Deep, racking sobs came then, dry and hard. He felt a terrible loneliness. He did not know what he was or what would become of him. He did not know what to do, where to go. All he knew was pain.

3:30

Exhausted, Jonathan could cry no more. He rolled over onto his back and realized he was still holding the gun. Slowly, he let it go. But his fingers, as if frozen in memory, remained tightly cramped and clawed, shaped like a shell over what they no longer held.

Lying on his back, Jonathan stared up at the overhanging trees, a laced and dark-green net. High above him the leaves constantly shifted, making a soft, hissing sound. He closed his eyes and shuddered.

3:35

Jonathan pushed himself to a sitting posture and looked about, wondering where he was. He tried to recall which direction he had come from, but could not. He pulled up his knees and, leaning forward, rested his chin on his arms. Tightly hugging himself, he rocked softly back and forth, sniffling.

His sleeve was torn. There was a smear of blood on his shoe. He touched the spot, finding it still sticky. He wondered whose blood it was.

"O God, O God, O God," he whispered. He had failed in all he had meant to do.

He was alive and wished that he was dead, but not being dead, he was scared that he might die.

3:38

Jonathan rubbed away his tears with the dirty heel of his hand. He blew his nose. He tried to move, to stand. When his weakened legs buckled, he reached for a tree. Fighting dizziness, he pulled himself up. He saw only bright, white points and flashes. He closed his eyes. Then, standing steadily at last, he opened them.

All around was woods. It was dark and seemed to be growing darker. He wondered what time it was, how many hours had passed.

As he turned around, his foot came up against his gun. He bent down and picked it up. For a moment he held it in his hands and just looked at it. Slowly, he released the flintlock. With an empty click it closed.

He relieved himself. Then he turned and tried to think of which way to go. What he wanted to do was run away, to go as far as possible and not return. But standing there, he heard a sound. Quickly he turned and saw a Hessian soldier standing not far off.

3:47

The grenadier was no more than thirty feet from Jonathan. Standing rigid, partially hidden by low branches, he was turning his head this way and that, as if he was searching for something.

Jonathan watched intently from behind a bush, certain the soldier was looking for him. He stared, trying to grasp the reality of what was happening. He could not. He knew that he had to do something, but he remained where he was, his gaze riveted by the Hessian's height, his bright uniform, the pale face beneath the high, golden cap. He seemed so powerful, holding his musket and bayonet in two large hands across his chest. He seemed enormous.

Why, Jonathan kept asking himself, is he looking for me? What have I done? Were all the others caught and am I, alone, still free? Why did the rest run? *Did* they run? Am I the only one alive?

The tall soldier, moving silently, took several steps in Jonathan's direction. Again he stopped and stared about. Then he turned his back on Jonathan, only to turn again.

Jonathan heard a crackling snap twenty feet in

another direction. Startled, he shifted his gaze. A second soldier was there. He was not quite as tall as the first, but fierce, with a sweeping mustache. He seemed older, too.

"*Siehst du was?*" the tall soldier called to the second.

The words astonished Jonathan. They had come so easily, so simply, yet he could not understand them at all.

Again, Jonathan told himself that he had to try and escape. Slowly, trying to make no noise, he squatted low and placed his gun on the ground. Pivoting on his heels, he looked behind him, hoping to find a way to go.

To his horror he discovered a third Hessian. He was completely surrounded.

3:50

"*Er erschiesst uns, wenn wir nicht vorsichtig sind,*" the new soldier said, speaking softly. He was much younger than the others, with a thin, blond wisp of mustache.

"*Weg von hier,*" said the older one. "*Es ist blöd und gefährlich. Wir finden ihn nie.*"

Jonathan closed his eyes and tried desperately to make some sense of the words.

"*Noch ein Paar Minuten,*" said the tall soldier.

"*Ich hab's satt,*" said the older.

Jonathan crouched low to the ground, certain the Hessians knew exactly where he was and that they were only deciding what to do with him.

The young soldier spoke again, but Jonathan could understand him no better than before. He watched their faces intently. Suddenly, he was sure he understood: They were going to kill him.

He jumped up. "Don't shoot!" he cried.

"*Mein Gott!*" the tall soldier cried. "*Vor unseren Augen!*"

"*Es ist nur ein Junge,*" said the young one.

Jonathan held his hands high over his head. "Don't kill me," he cried. "Please!"

The soldiers leveled their guns at him. The older one spoke, and they looked about as if in search of others. Apparently satisfied no one else was there, they scrutinized Jonathan. He couldn't bear their stares. Hanging his head, he began to cry, slowly sinking to his knees, as the sobs deepened. He felt numb and utterly helpless.

"Komm hierher!" the old soldier shouted at him.

Trying to stifle his cries, Jonathan looked up. He knew he was being told to do something. And he wanted more than anything to do it, but he didn't understand what it was.

"Idiot!" cried the soldier. *"Die verstehen nie. Komm hierher, Junge."*

Jonathan pushed himself to his feet, then took a tentative step toward the one who had been speaking to him.

The soldier nodded. *"Das ist besser,"* he said.

Encouraged by the man's tone, Jonathan took another cautious step. Again the soldier nodded. With increasing relief that he was doing the right thing, Jonathan continued to move. But the soldier suddenly shouted at him and hastily lifted his gun. *"Halt!"*

Jonathan stopped at once. From either side the other two soldiers moved closer. The tall one stepped on the gun Jonathan had left. With a cry, he snatched it up and held it triumphantly aloft. The soldiers talked to one another.

Not moving, afraid to look about, aware only that they were talking about him, Jonathan said, "I don't know what you want me to do."

The youngest of the soldiers looked at him curiously. *"Wir sprechen kein Englisch,"* he said. *"Warum sprichst du kein Deutsch?"*

The other soldiers laughed.

Baffled, Jonathan kept studying their faces, trying to find some clue to their words. The tall one had a scar by his cheek. The old one kept touching his mustache, while the youngest had bright, rosy cheeks. Now and again as they talked, they looked at Jonathan. Then one of them laughed and the others joined in. Feeling shame, certain they were making fun of him, Jonathan hung his head.

"Dreh dich um!" the older soldier barked.

Startled, Jonathan looked up.

"Dreh dich um!" the Hessian repeated, clearly exasperated. Reaching out, he shoved Jonathan. Taken by surprise, Jonathan tripped and fell, instantly covering his head with his arms to ward off the blow he sensed was to follow.

"Los," said the older one, *"er macht vor Angst in die Hosen."*

The young one gave him an answer.

Jonathan, sure they were about to do something to him, shut his eyes tightly. But when nothing happened, he opened them again. They were only studying him, the muzzles of their guns pointing toward the ground.

"*Steh auf!*" the older one snapped. "*Es tut dir keiner was.*" Reaching down, he pulled at Jonathan's arm and hauled him to his feet. Then he shoved him—this time not so hard—in the direction he wanted the boy to move. Jonathan began to walk shakily. Behind, the three soldiers followed.

4:01

"*Warte!*" said the older soldier, putting a hand to Jonathan's shoulder. The trees had begun to thin. The old soldier swung a pack from his back onto the ground, opened it, and pulled out a rope. He slapped Jonathan's arms up and tied the rope around his waist, then handed the free end to the youngest Hessian. Leaving Jonathan with the young soldier, the two others went forward.

Jonathan looked down at the rope, then at the soldier, who was holding it and watching him. The soldier gave a shrug and looked about.

"*Es ist ein schönes Land,*" he said after a moment.

Though Jonathan didn't know what he meant, it sounded kindly.

Jonathan looked more closely at him. He wondered just how old he was. It occurred to him that he might be the same age as his older brother. He tried to picture the young Hessian's home. It was impossible. All he could see was his own home.

Noting Jonathan's gaze, the soldier smiled. It made his cheeks even brighter. *"Soldat,"* he said, pointing first to himself, then to Jonathan.

"Soldat," Jonathan repeated, nodding to show he understood. "Soldier," he said more slowly in reply, suddenly hearing it as an echo of what he had wanted to be. "Soldier," he said softly, realizing that indeed, that was what he now was. *"Soldat . . ."* he whispered, feeling his intense humiliation.

The Hessian only grinned at the repetition of words.

Jonathan peered up into his face. The smile seemed to mock him. He suddenly felt hatred. He wanted to cry again.

A call came from the two who had gone ahead. The soldier's smile vanished. *"Los, geh!"* he said sharply, and shook the rope.

Jonathan felt a sharp pain in the area of his heart.

4:10

Within moments they had stepped out onto the road.

Jonathan realized that it was the same ground where the fighting had occurred. It was completely deserted now. The only evidence of what had happened there was bits of cartridge paper caught in the grass by the edge of the road.

Then Jonathan noticed a dark stain in the middle of the road. He wondered if it might be blood. Was it where his father's friend had fallen? The Frenchman? The Hessian? Where had the bodies gone? Who had taken them? He felt abandoned, totally alone. With a shock, he realized that he had expected to see the other Hessians. But they too were gone. *Where?*

The three Hessians were standing together, deep in conversation, the younger one still holding the rope.

Jonathan tried to rekindle his hatred, but all he could muster was the desire to stand close to them, to be taken care of. He didn't want to be left out. But they were paying no attention to him. Instead, they were looking up and down the road, the tall one pointing in various directions.

Thunder rumbled and rain began falling on Jonathan's face. With a jerk the older soldier grabbed the rope away from the younger one and marched Jonathan along the road with them. They moved in the direction the Hessians had originally come from, toward Pennington. As they went, they tried to keep under branches, away from the rain.

A stroke of lightning flashed, followed by heavy thunder. Rain poured down in gray sheets. They moved closer to the trees but still didn't escape getting drenched. The soldiers wrapped pieces of cloth around their flintlocks but didn't bother with Jonathan's gun.

It was the young soldier who discovered the great pine tree, its lowest branches four feet off the ground. Beneath was an open space blanketed with a mass of brown pine needles. The soldier took off his cap and crawled in, pulling his gun after him. The other two soldiers, roughly pushing Jonathan ahead, followed.

The four of them, not speaking, sat and waited, listening. The rain fell steadily, broken occasionally by thunder and lightning. The old soldier took out a pipe, but having no light, merely sucked on the stem.

The sound of the beating rain filled Jonathan with sorrow. The wash of water seemed to obliterate him. Though he tried not to, he began to think of what the Hessians might yet do to him. He wished he knew.

4:30

Though the torrential rains slackened off and the darkness lightened, a steady drizzle continued. From time to time the soldiers spoke to one another. Jonathan tried to listen, hoping to hear words that would make some sense, but finding very few.

Carefully, furtively, he studied their faces, trying to guess their thoughts and moods. The older one worried him most. His mustache made him appear very angry; his manner was tense. The tall one looked menacing because of his giant size and his scar. The young one, however, seemed safer. He wondered how much he should trust him.

Jonathan wished he could talk to them, do something so they would not hurt him. Though for the moment they weren't acting as if they were going to harm him, Jonathan recalled stories he had heard about what happened to prisoners. Hessians had a reputation for being vicious. Some prisoners, his father had told him, were hanged as rebels. Some were placed in jails or in the dreadful hulks of prison ships. Jonathan had a memory too that some prisoners were sold into slavery, or sent to distant places, never allowed to come home. He wished he had paid attention to such tales. He knew so little, so very little!

He began to wonder about what truly had happened when they had fought. He knew they had been beaten. It had been so confused, so wrongly done, it was a wonder that they had even stood and fought at all. It seemed so stupid now.

Perhaps others had been taken prisoner too. He hoped they had. It would make him feel better, knowing that he was not the only one.

He would have liked to be able to ask the Hessians what had happened. But they were ignoring him completely, silently watching the rain as it continued to taper off. And watching their stony faces, still trying to read their thoughts, Jonathan grew sleepy.

5:00

"Steh auf!"

Roughly shaken, Jonathan opened his eyes. The tall Hessian was leaning over him. With a rush Jonathan remembered where he was and what had happened.

Again the soldier called to him, gesturing.

One by one they crawled from beneath the pine boughs and stood up.

The grass underfoot, the branches, the bark, the leaves, all held a soaking sheen. A gray-green mist filled the wooded air with a soft half-light, making the surrounding trees rise up like vaulting shadows. There was no edge to things. It was impossible to see far. They might have been at the very center of the world, or near the end. From somewhere hidden, but nearby, a woodpecker worked with a *rat-ta-tat*.

They moved from the woods back onto the muddy road. Jonathan, still held at the end of the slack rope by the older soldier, felt the water that had soaked through his shoes making his feet cold. He was very hungry.

On the road the soldiers hesitated. Quietly,

uneasily, they talked amongst themselves. The tall one spoke least of all.

They began to walk down the middle of the road, keeping Jonathan in their midst. They talked very little now, but it was clear to Jonathan from their cautious looking around that they were wary, and not at all sure of where they were going, or what they might meet. Now and again they paused to look and listen. There was little to hear, less to see. The world had grown very small.

Every time they paused, Jonathan paused. When they moved, he moved. At one point, when the young soldier stopped to look at something by the road, Jonathan did the same. But when the older soldier did not stop, the suddenly taut rope made Jonathan slip and fall into the mud.

As he pulled himself up and wiped his face, the Hessians laughed. Jonathan started to laugh too, but then his terrible shame returned. In an instant, the weight of his failures dropped over him again like an eyeless hood. The Hessians, unaware, moved on.

Jonathan began to feel that he was walking into a nightmare, that he had entered a world other than the one he knew. Then, with a shock he realized he had not been thinking of trying to escape. He looked up sharply. The old soldier, rope in hand, was paying scant attention. A sudden break and he could free himself. That he had not been thinking of getting away embarassed him. *Escape* . . . wouldn't a true soldier be thinking of that? Why, he kept asking himself, hadn't *he*?

But even as he asked, he understood. If he escaped, where would he go? To his father, who had not wanted him to leave? To his mother, to whom he had not listened? To the tavern keeper, who had warned him, and to whom he'd given his word he'd return the gun? To the Americans, who would mock him? To the Corporal? He had failed them all! As he pictured each face, it broke apart, until there seemed nothing left of his past.

Jonathan looked at the soldiers. And they, he asked himself, were they his only friends?

5:15

"Wir haben uns verirrt," said the young soldier. They had all come to a halt and were looking about.

Jonathan gazed up at the one who had spoken.

He could see that he was puzzled, worried. The others acted just as perplexed.

"Vielleicht sind wir geschlagen. Vielleicht sind wir die einzigen am Leben!"

"Gott helf uns!"

Jonathan, wondering what they said, saw only worry on their faces. The young one kept fingering his thin mustache. The tall one rubbed the scar. It seemed to bother him. Perhaps, thought Jonathan, it was the dampness. Like his father's leg.

The Hessians talked amongst themselves again, keeping their voices low as if they might be overheard. As they gazed now one way, now another, Jonathan watched intently. He decided they did not know which way to go.

5:20

They continued to walk slowly and close together. Jonathan, chilled and damp, made no resistance to the chafing rope. The fog, sometimes thin, sometimes dense, floated before them, around them, over them, like some living thing.

71

"O Gott!" cried the tall soldier, flinging up an arm to stop them.

Instantly, the two other soldiers brought their guns about and stared where the tall one pointed. Jonathan, as frightened as they, looked too. What he saw was there and then not there, moving so quickly in and out of sight as to make him uncertain he had seen anything at all. He thought it had been a man, and even in that briefest second believed it had been the Corporal. But the figure had vanished so quickly in the fog that it was impossible for Jonathan to be sure.

"Es ist nichts," said the young soldier. He laughed with nervous relief.

"Doch, da war was!" said the tall one with indignation.

His heart beating rapidly, Jonathan turned about, wondering if there were other Americans near. He saw not the slightest clue. Nor did he know how he felt, glad or sorry. Before he could consider some action, he felt the rope about his waist jerk as the old soldier hauled him in closer.

The soldiers, standing still, seemed to be growing more nervous. They talked quietly but with great urgency one to the other.

Jonathan, his head hurting from being unable to

decide what to do, closed his eyes. When he opened them, he saw that the soldiers were standing absolutely still, straining to listen.

Nothing.

The fog settled deeper.

The older soldier finally said something. To Jonathan, it sounded like a curse. Whatever it was, the other two agreed. They all began to move again.

Jonathan looked back. Glad or sorry? His head seemed to throb with it. *Glad or sorry?* He did not know.

5:30

From somewhere they could hear the lowing call of a cow. At once they stopped. It was a plaintive sound, like a signal of distress. They faced the direction from which it came.

The sound repeated, low and just as mournful.

Without saying anything to one another, the Hessians began to move in the direction of the sound, crossing the road and entering the dark, soaking woods.

Keeping Jonathan close, they moved with elaborate care. When the cow lowed again, closer yet, they halted. Jonathan wondered at the sound. That it was a cow in distress he had no doubt. He wondered if the Hessians could, or would, understand. Did they, he asked himself, have cows in the land they came from?

The tall soldier unwrapped his gun, primed it anew, then wrapped it up quickly once more. To his pack he affixed Jonathan's gun so it was secure and out of the way.

It was almost impossible to see anything. Still, they stood there, waiting for another call from the cow. The sound of dripping water made Jonathan tense.

When the call did come, it seemed closer than it had before. Jonathan felt relieved.

The soldiers turned and began to hurry. Within minutes they came up against a rail fence and what appeared in the fog to be an open space beyond.

Again the cow called, but they could not see across the field.

The other two soldiers brought their guns around and checked the priming. Once more Jonathan thought about the Corporal and the other Americans. Perhaps they were close, even across the field.

Should he send out a warning call? Who was he more afraid of, the Hessians or the Americans?

The soldiers climbed the fence. Jonathan attempted to follow, only to become entangled in the rope. The young soldier leaned over the top rail and began to untie the rope. The old one, seeing what was happening, glared at the young soldier, but then turned back across the field, distracted, when the cow bleated again. The young soldier pulled away the rope. Slowly, Jonathan climbed the fence and joined the Hessians.

As they began to cross over the spongy pasture ground, the old soldier made Jonathan walk in front.

In the open area the fog grew thinner. The Hessians kept a few paces apart, their muskets ready, their bayonets fixed as if they were advancing on an enemy.

Jonathan stared in the direction they were moving, hoping he would see whatever they were approaching first.

The fog lifted some more and Jonathan saw the cow. A rope, broken, dangled from her neck. Beyond the cow was a dark house.

5:40

The house was smaller than Jonathan's own. Swedish style, it was made of logs, chinked with decaying clay, and clogged with clods of moss. In front of the doorway a shallow covered porch ran the full width of the house. It looked deserted, containing no sense of light or life. The cow, standing before the closed door, kept lifting her head, stretching, and lowing. Not far from the house, off to one side, was a smaller building, whose double doors were also closed.

With great care, their boots sticking in the wet ground, they continued to advance, Jonathan still in front of the Hessians. When they came close to the house, they stopped.

The cow swung her head up and around, looking at them, her tongue flicking. Again she called, deep and long. Jonathan understood that she was waiting to be milked, waiting for someone to come from the house. But no one did.

Unsure what to do, the soldiers stood still, exchanging anxious glances. The young one and the tall one kept looking to the oldest, waiting for him to make up his mind. It was he, finally, who touched

Jonathan on the arm. *"Los!"* he said, pushing him forward. *"Mach die Tür auf."*

Jonathan took a few tentative steps forward, then stopped and turned. He looked at the young soldier, but he was impassive. The old soldier waved his arm, and Jonathan understood him to mean that he should continue. Just to be certain, he took three more steps then turned yet again. The soldier nodded.

Jonathan stepped on the porch. It sagged slightly. Using a post, he pulled himself up and listened.

Nothing.

Approaching the door, he reached out a hand, withdrew it, and gazed back toward the soldiers.

"Los!" came the impatient, whispered command. The old one lifted his gun. Jonathan heard the click as he drew back his flintlock.

Nervously, Jonathan knocked timidly on the door.

"Noch einmal!" the older soldier called in a hoarse whisper.

A second knock. Still no answer. Finally, Jonathan reached for the latch, squeezed it, then pushed. The door, swinging on old hinges, opened halfway. Jonathan glanced back. The Hessians, who had advanced a few more paces, urged him on.

Carefully, Jonathan pushed the door completely open and stepped inside.

It was a one-room house with a dirt floor, one oil-papered window, and a hearth at the far side. A table stood in the middle of the room. One low counter—Jonathan thought it a bed—was against the wall. Two old chairs. A number of boxes against the walls. On the table a few things that had been left: a cup, a tin plate, a candle in a stand. A wooden shovel stood by the door. It was a poor house, a meager house with the look of having been quickly abandoned.

Jonathan turned to the door as the tall soldier came in, his great size filling the doorframe. Within moments the other two entered.

The young soldier began to poke about. When he found a half loaf of bread, he flung it on the table, where it landed with a dull thump.

Outside the cow bleated.

"It wants milking," said Jonathan.

"Was war das?" the young soldier said to him.

The tall soldier spoke curtly. To Jonathan they all seemed angry, frustrated.

Again the cow called.

"Milking," Jonathan said, speaking carefully, first pointing outside, then making milking motions with his hands. "You can drink it," he said, making a drinking motion.

The young soldier looked at him quizzically, until, with sudden comprehension, he laughed. *"Melken!"* he cried. *"Wir können dann die Milch trinken."*

Thinking he had made himself understood, Jonathan cast about for a bucket, but couldn't find one. The young soldier, not understanding, pushed him encouragingly toward the door.

Jonathan went. The soldier stood watching him from the doorway.

Once outside, Jonathan moved to the cow and stroked her about her ears, still searching about for a bucket. Remembering the shed he had seen off to one side, he caught the soldier's attention and pointed toward it.

The soldier winked at him from the porch where he stood.

The wink made Jonathan grin, and filled him with a sense of camaraderie. Feeling good, almost happy, he walked across the way and pulled the shed doors open. He looked inside.

Sitting on the ground was a child.

6:00

The child was very young—Jonathan could see that. His own sister was seven years old and this boy was not close to her in size. He sat on the ground, his feet bare, his linsey-woolsey blouse veined with dirt, his dark face caked with mud. His arms and legs were filthy.

When Jonathan first looked in, the boy, as if coming from sleep, lifted sudden, startled eyes, opening his mouth as if to speak, but then said nothing.

Jonathan quickly glanced toward the house. The young soldier was standing on the porch, staring into the distance beyond the shed. He did not notice Jonathan.

Jonathan turned back to the boy.

"Don't talk!" he whispered quickly as he put a hand to the boy's mouth.

The boy pulled his head back and gazed dumbly at Jonathan.

Jonathan returned the look, trying to understand his own feelings, which were now in a jumble again. Should he tell the Hessians what he had found or not?

He glanced about the shed. A window, no more than a hole under the eaves, let in enough light for him to see that the shed contained only a few implements, a pile of straw, and in a corner a wooden bucket. He decided he needed time to think what to do.

He reached for the bucket, and though he wasn't close, the little boy shied away at once.

"Where are your parents?" Jonathan asked, keeping his voice as low as possible.

The boy stared at him. His stillness frightened Jonathan. It reminded him that he was a prisoner. He looked back at the house. The soldier was still not watching.

"Your mother and father," said Jonathan urgently, "are they hiding? Are they near?"

The boy gave no response. Impulsively, as if to see if he was real, Jonathan reached out to touch him again. The boy shied away.

"Are they close?" Jonathan asked, more gently this time. When he received no answer, he stood up and peeked out of the shed. Now the soldier was looking in his direction.

"*Los, geh!*" the Hessian shouted.

"I have to milk the cow," said Jonathan to the boy. "Just stay here. Don't you move. I'll be back as fast as I can." Snatching up the bucket, he slipped out of the shed, carefully leaving the doors just slightly ajar.

Acutely aware that the young soldier was now observing him, and wondering if he suspected anything, Jonathan went to the cow. He didn't look at the Hessian. He placed the bucket under the cow's udder, then quickly knelt, pressing his face against the warm flanks. The cow stamped. Jonathan began to milk.

The milk came in hard streams, foaming white and frothy. Working rhythmically, Jonathan shut his eyes and felt the rough, warm hide against his face. Milking was one of his tasks at home, and the familiar pattern of sound soothed him.

He thought of the little boy. Who was he? What was he doing there? Where was the rest of his family? Should he tell the Hessians, and if he did what would they do? They had seemed friendly enough— were they truly?

After filling the bucket, Jonathan moved away so the cow wouldn't kick it over.

The young soldier, watching, mumbled his approval. Jonathan guiltily averted his eyes.

He brought the bucket into the house.

The candle had been lit. The tall soldier was sprawled on the bed, his long arms and legs dangling to the floor. The old Hessian, his jacket loosened and sash undone, sat at the table, toying with the small cup. Jonathan was reminded again how big they all were.

The bread had been cut into three large pieces and one smaller one.

Jonathan set the milk bucket on the table, now very much aware of his hunger. He stared at the bread. The old soldier, noticing, pushed the smallest piece toward him, then made motions to the cup with his hand.

Jonathan wasn't sure what he was supposed to do. The Hessian mimicked his earlier drinking movement. Thankful, Jonathan filled the cup with milk by dipping it into the bucket, then drew it out and drank it down in two quick swallows. The old soldier gave an approving grunt. Jonathan filled the cup a second time, and was about to take it for himself when he saw the Hessian's hand extended. He handed the full cup to him. The Hessian drained it. Then the young soldier came and helped himself, only to hand the cup back to the older one, who continued drinking.

When the tall one roused himself for his portion, the young one went to the hearth and attempted to get a fire started.

Jonathan, having bolted his bread to satisfy his immediate hunger, now was impatient to leave the house and get back to the boy. He tried to think of some excuse to go, then considered whether or not he should tell the soldiers. He wanted to.

The cow began to low again. The soldiers ignored it until, when it persisted, the young one stood up and waved Jonathan toward the bucket and the door.

Jonathan moved slowly. He picked up the bucket and started for the door. There he paused to see if anyone would follow. Casually, the young soldier stood and lumbered after.

Jonathan milked the cow again. The bucket filled more slowly this time. As Jonathan worked, he kept going over what to do in his mind. More than once he glanced up at the soldier, who was hardly keeping any watch on him at all. One moment Jonathan wanted to tell him. The next moment he did not, confused anew about whether the Hessians were his friends or enemies.

When he obviously could get no more milk from the cow, Jonathan stood up.

"*Fertig?*" asked the Hessian.

"I have to take care of the cow," said Jonathan, almost without thinking, and handed the bucket to the soldier. He pointed to the cow, then to the shed. Comprehending, the soldier shrugged, then turned and took the bucket inside, leaving Jonathan alone.

For a moment Jonathan just stood there, taking in deeply the realization that the young soldier was completely trusting him. Uneasy, he grabbed hold of the rope, which was dangling from the cow's neck, and led her toward the shed.

6:30

The cow went docilely, without complaint. At the shed door Jonathan tied the rope to a post and, with a quick glance back over his shoulder, carefully opened the door. The boy was still there. He looked up at Jonathan.

Jonathan sidled in, angling the door so that if one of the soldiers came out on the porch, he would not be able to see in, yet leaving enough of an opening to allow some light. He squatted by the boy's side.

"Where are your parents?" he whispered, repeating the question he had asked before. "I need to know."

The boy only looked at him through the dim light.

Jonathan studied his face as if the puzzle could be untangled there. The boy's eyes were tired, his mouth a soft, tremulous frown. His dreary sadness made Jonathan uneasy. Something had happened.

"Your parents," Jonathan tried, urgency returning to his voice. "Your mother. Is she coming back? Mama?"

A flicker of understanding sparked the boy's eyes. His mouth twitched slightly. His face softened. For a moment Jonathan thought the boy might cry. Then, in a tentative gesture, the boy lifted a hand and pointed.

Jonathan looked where the boy had pointed. It made no sense. Deciding that he simply could not understand, that he needed help, that he had to trust the Hessians, he put out his hand. "Come with me," he said. The boy did nothing.

Jonathan stood up, his hand again reaching out. "Come with me," he repeated, speaking more gently.

Cautiously, the boy put out his hand. Jonathan took it and led him out of the shed.

Approaching the house, holding the boy firmly by the hand, Jonathan crossed over to the porch, to the door. There he paused briefly before going inside.

6:35

It was the old soldier who saw them first. *"Mein Gott!"* he cried.

The tone of his voice brought the other two around, one from his resting place on the bed, the other from the hearth. They all looked down at the boy. Never had the soldiers seemed more enormous to Jonathan than they did then.

"Woher kommt denn der?" asked the young soldier.

"He was in the shed," Jonathan replied, not knowing if he was answering the question. "He was just sitting there. I asked him where his parents were. He won't answer."

The Hessians exchanged glances. Then the young one shrugged and laughed and returned to his bed, while the tall one, frowning, went back to the hearth. The old one took up his seat at the table and kept rubbing a hand along his mustache.

The boy had not moved, clearly preferring to stay with Jonathan.

"Can you tell me where your mother is?" Jonathan asked the boy. Then, remembering that he had responded to the word "Mama," he used it.

Again there was a reaction. The boy looked around as if trying to gain a sense of direction. At last he pointed.

The young soldier had propped himself up on one elbow. *"Was sagt er?"* he asked.

"Your mama," Jonathan repeated directly into the boy's face and speaking very slowly. "Where? *Mama?*"

For a moment the boy gazed at Jonathan, and then began to tug at him. Jonathan allowed himself to be led toward the door. There he stopped and, with a look, appealed to the Hessians. The two turned to the older one who, scowling, stood up. As Jonathan, led by the boy, went out, the soldiers followed.

6:45

Jonathan found the boy's parents out beyond a small field, not far from the rear loop of the fence. It was an area where the woods had started to reclaim the land.

A man—Jonathan assumed it was the boy's father—lay on his back, his arms wide to either side, his eyes closed, dead. The woman, also dead, lay face downward. Their clothing was wet, torn, pink with blood. The woman's hair, long and gray, draped over her neck like a fringed shawl.

For a moment the boy simply stood next to the bodies. Then he sat down and began to play with his mother's hair, attempting with awkward fingers to braid it. His face was blank.

Jonathan was deeply shaken, unwilling to accept what was before his eyes. How could this happen? Who could have done it?

The three Hessians approached, carrying their guns. Their uniforms were in disarray.

Seeing the bodies, they stopped short. Jonathan scrutinized the soldiers' faces. Mostly, they seemed to show annoyance. He felt a sudden spasm of anger: Why didn't they react more?

"Are these your parents?" Jonathan asked the boy. His voice seemed too loud. The boy lifted his face. "What happened?" Jonathan asked.

The boy, either not comprehending or unable to say, gave no reply.

"Can't you speak?" Jonathan pleaded.

The boy did not.

Jonathan glanced behind at the soldiers. They had kept their distance. Jonathan looked about the area in which they were standing, the encroaching trees, the field beyond. The darkness had thickened. The sky had almost disappeared. For what he could see of the rest of the world, they might have been on an island. Behind him the three soldiers, clearly impatient, shifted uneasily. A gentle breeze stirred the trees.

With a look, Jonathan tried to appeal to the young soldier. But he only shook his head, muttered something under his breath, then turned and went back to the house. The tall one followed.

With growing dismay, Jonathan gazed at the bodies, at the boy, at the remaining soldier, the old one.

Reaching out, the Hessian clapped a hand on Jonathan's shoulder, gave him a shake, and nodded toward the house. Then he walked off a few paces.

The boy's fingers were woven into his mother's wet hair.

Jonathan looked at the Hessian, who stood waiting. *"Nun komm!"* he called, his face glowering with impatience. As though taking a leap, Jonathan suddenly found an answer to his questions.

He turned back to the boy. "Did *they* kill them?" he whispered breathlessly.

The boy remained immobile.

"I need to know," demanded Jonathan, feeling the dread of coming upon an awful truth. "Do you recognize them?"

Again he looked back at the old soldier, recalling—with an avalanche of associations—all the stories he had heard about Hessian brutality. He saw the Hessians again as they were on the road, at the fighting place. He saw too his father's friend, dead. He could see the Frenchman with his shaking, bleeding head. To the boy he said, "They were the ones, weren't they?"

"Komm!" shouted the soldier angrily. The sharp command felt like the cut of a whip stroke.

"Come with me," Jonathan said to the boy.

Taking the boy by the hand, he followed the old soldier back to the house.

7:00

The young soldier was lying on the bed, his arms thrown over his eyes, his bootless feet dangling over one end. The tall soldier was sitting near the fire, which he had managed to light, his head nodding as he tried to fend off sleep. The old one, who had entered ahead of Jonathan, had taken his place at the table and had already started to work on his pipe, trying to light it. The pipe was like a toy in his large hands.

Jonathan, the boy at his side, stood by the door and looked in. He could feel the press of his rising anger. The soldiers' callousness gave more and more strength to his conviction that they had been party to the killing. But even as he believed it, he did not want to believe it. He wanted, yearningly, to give them a chance to prove him wrong.

"They need to be buried," he said out loud.

None of the soldiers paid any attention. The old soldier puffed a cloud of smoke.

Jonathan went to where the young soldier lay.

"They need to be buried," he repeated. "I can't do it alone."

When the young soldier gave no response, Jonathan put out a hand and tentatively shook the man's arm. The Hessian swatted at him and rolled over so that his back was to Jonathan.

Hurt by the rebuff, Jonathan turned around. The tall soldier was now stretched out full length, asleep. Only the old soldier was awake.

For a long while Jonathan stood there, trying to calm his thoughts, which pulled him first one way, then another.

"Did you do it?" he suddenly blurted out.

The old soldier puffed his pipe. Behind the smoke the expression on his face seemed lost, vague, absent.

Seething, Jonathan turned abruptly and grabbed the shovel that was by the door. He held it up so the soldier would see it.

"I'm going to bury them," he said.

For a moment the old soldier's eyes looked up, but then became indifferent again. Jonathan took the boy's hand and returned to where the bodies lay.

The boy watched intently. But whether he understood what was about to happen, Jonathan could not tell.

Jonathan began to dig alongside the couple, as if he were trying to burst the ground open. The thickly knotted roots and the dull shovel blade conspired against him. Enraged, he chopped into the earth. Then, desperately trying to control himself, he recollected how he had worked his father's fields. Pressing his foot against the top of the shovel, he flung his full weight down onto it, forcing the blade into the earth. He dug more and more furiously as the ground began to give way.

And the little boy watched.

7:35

Jonathan dug until he could not dig anymore. Yet he knew the grave was too narrow and not nearly deep enough. The boy, his head resting on his mother's hair, had fallen asleep.

Jonathan knew he had to get help. He was exhausted and covered with a damp, unclean sweat. He could do no more. He returned to the house, shovel in hand, his fury unspent.

In the house it was as before: Only the old one was awake. He was sitting with his big feet up on the table. Crumbs from the loaf of bread were before him. The cup lay in a small pool of blue-white milk. The bucket was almost empty.

"I need some help," Jonathan said brusquely. He held up the shovel.

Gradually, the soldier lifted his head and stared at Jonathan. His face took Jonathan by surprise. He hadn't fully realized until then how old the man was. It was as if the fierce mustache was a disguise. Now he saw that much of his hair was gray, and the day-old stubble of whitish beard on his face made him seem older yet. His eyes were tired.

"I can't do it myself," said Jonathan, suddenly feeling defeated. "I need help," he repeated, pleading.

Slowly, stiffly, the man got up and went over to where the young soldier was sleeping. He shook him hard and spoke sharply.

The young soldier sat up, looking first at the old soldier and then at Jonathan. Again the old soldier spoke. To Jonathan, it sounded as if he was giving commands.

Sullenly, the young soldier swung about, groped for his boots, and pulled them on.

Jonathan, shovel in hand, stood by the door, waiting.

Staggering slightly from sleepiness, the young soldier came to the door, looked out, and saw that it had become dark. He went back to catch up a burning brand from the fire.

Torch held high, the Hessian followed Jonathan. It wasn't a bright flame, only a feeble, orange light, fussing and spitting in the damp air. It seemed to make the darkness darker.

7:40

Jonathan led the way. He found the boy where he had left him, asleep beside his parents.

The young soldier stopped and looked at what Jonathan had done. Speaking sharply, with obvious disgust, he thrust the burning stick into Jonathan's hand and snatched up the shovel. Jonathan, terrified for a moment that the soldier was going to strike him, jumped back.

But the young soldier only stood in the shallow grave and began to dig hurriedly, throwing out the dirt while talking in muttering tones to himself, and giving Jonathan angry looks. Jonathan's own anger returned. He stood stonily by. When the young soldier tired—which was soon—he flipped the shovel to Jonathan and climbed out.

Jonathan let himself down into the grave and began to dig again, but the young soldier impatiently jumped back in, took back the shovel, and fairly flung Jonathan out of the way.

"Das genügt," the Hessian finally said with a dusting of his hands. Throwing the shovel out, he hauled himself up.

Jonathan went to the boy and gently tried to rouse him. At first he would not waken, until, with a jerk of his head, he sat up, shying from Jonathan's touch. The boy's eyes moved from him to the young soldier and widened. Jonathan looked around. The young soldier was holding the burning stick high, making the shadows on his face long and severe, as if his head had been stretched. Jonathan saw him in a new way—powerful and evil.

The Hessian stuck the stick into the ground so that it stood like a candle. Then he went to the man's feet. *"Halt ihn fest,"* he said curtly to Jonathan.

Jonathan went to the man's arms. After a moment's hesitation, he braced himself and gripped the man's wrists. The skin was cold and stiff. The boy, sitting on the ground, watched, wide-eyed.

First they turned the man into the grave. Then they moved the woman. She rolled in, landing upon the man on her back. For the first time Jonathan saw her face. Her mouth was open, her eyes closed, her sallow face smeared with dirt. Her teeth were large and crooked, eyeteeth missing. Her bloodless lips were drawn back, and Jonathan could see her tongue. It was black.

"Los, beeil dich!" the young soldier commanded. He reached down and grabbed a handful of dirt, which he tossed onto the couple. Then he pointed at Jonathan and made hurried motions with his hand.

Jonathan reluctantly picked up the shovel. Taking earth from the pile that had been made, he began to cover the bodies. When the dirt hit the woman's face and went into her open mouth, he stopped, trying to catch his breath. Then he turned and retched.

Trembling, he turned back to the grave. The young soldier grabbed the shovel from him and flung in the rest of the dirt. Jonathan stood aside, ashamed.

When the grave was filled, the young soldier tossed the shovel aside and then pointed to the watching boy, making a rising gesture with his hand.

Jonathan crossed over and pulled the boy to his feet. This time the boy came willingly and stood close by. But when Jonathan tried to take his hand, he snatched it away and made a fist. Jonathan fought back his tears. It was for his own sake he wished to hold the boy's hand.

The young soldier closed two of his jacket buttons and touched his thin mustache as if to straighten it, an imitation of the gesture Jonathan had seen the old soldier make many times. Then, standing a little straighter, the soldier began to speak. Because of the singsong cadence, Jonathan sensed it was a prayer and wished he knew its meaning.

Finishing quickly—all too quickly in Jonathan's judgment—the young soldier wiped his hands on his jacket, then, picking up the torch, made a motion to Jonathan that they were to return to the house. Jonathan looked over his shoulder. He could see the glowing oil-paper window.

When he bent over to pick up the boy, the boy resisted. But this time Jonathan clung to him, knowing that he needed to hold the child. The young soldier started off. Jonathan followed, feeling the soft, steady, and comforting breath of the boy against his neck.

8:15

Once in the house, Jonathan set the boy on the floor. The young soldier went straight to where he had been before, pulled off his boots, and lay down. Within moments he was asleep.

The tall soldier sprawled before the fire, his long body stretched full length, his head cradled in one arm. His other, fisted hand was pressed against his mouth like a child's. Occasionally, he snored.

The old soldier remained awake. Sitting on the ground, he had wedged himself into a corner, pipe in hand. From it a thin line of smoke rose. He seemed to deliberately avoid looking at Jonathan or the boy.

Jonathan looked at the soldiers, feeling miserable and bitter. Then he poured out the last cup of milk and gave it to the boy, who, holding the cup in two hands, drained it slowly. When he was done, he gave the cup back, then gazed about as if in search of something. After a moment he pointed across the room and tugged at Jonathan's leg. At first Jonathan wasn't sure what he wanted. Then he saw that there was a long, boxlike object under the young soldier's bed.

Jonathan pulled it out. The box contained a linen sack filled with straw. There was also a blanket. It was the boy's bed.

The boy helped him drag it along the floor, guiding it until it sat directly under the table. The boy got in. Turning on his side, he pulled the blanket up and simply lay there, staring at the side of the box.

Jonathan watched. Then he reached in and briefly touched the nape of the boy's neck, where the hair was soft. The boy shifted slightly, then lay still.

Jonathan stood up. Once again he glanced about the room, his eyes meeting the old soldier's. The Hessian beckoned to him. As Jonathan nervously approached him, he realized that the Hessian was holding the rope. As soon as Jonathan was close enough, the Hessian leaned forward and quickly tied the rope around Jonathan's ankle, then tied a tight knot. Jonathan saw that the other end of the rope was fastened to the soldier's ankle.

The old soldier shifted about and smoked his pipe indifferently.

Jonathan suddenly felt his own weariness. He sat down as far away from the Hessian as the rope would allow, and with his back to him.

He looked down at the rope, which pinched

101

tightly. In a glance he saw that it was a knot he could untie.

He felt his heart begin to beat rapidly.

He quickly glanced about the room. The old soldier's head was now bent back against the wall, his chest moving with the deep rhythm of sleep. His mouth was slightly agape. From his hand the pipe dangled and then fell, spilling sparks of red ash so that for a moment the earth floor glowed like a deep, star-filled sky.

Jonathan studied the other sleeping men. He swung about on his knees and saw the boy, who was also asleep.

Keeping an eye on the old soldier, Jonathan tentatively plucked at the rope that held him. Then, working with increasing sureness, he looked down and used both hands. The knot fell open.

Jonathan stood up, listening to the night sounds—peepers, an owl. The scurrying of something on the roof above. He remained motionless, as if waiting for something to happen.

Gradually, it came to him that he could do anything, anything he chose to do. The soldiers, all asleep, were powerless. He could, he knew, simply walk away and be free. He could stay and be their prisoner. Or—he realized with a quickening sense of dread—he could do what any true soldier would do. He could kill them.

8:45

"Do it," he whispered to himself. "Do it. . . ." His eyes searched the room for the muskets. He found them in a corner, neatly stacked, the Hessians' caps nearby.

Caught between the hatred he felt toward the soldiers and his fear, he remained unmoving. "Do it," his own voice told himself. "Do what soldiers do . . . pick up the gun . . . make them pay for what they've done. . . ."

He forced himself to look at the old soldier. "He's cruel," he told himself, "a murderer . . . an enemy."

Silently, Jonathan moved across the room and picked up his own gun. Remembering how wet it had gotten, he set it back down and picked up one of the Hessians' guns. It lay across his hands. "Do it," he heard himself say yet again. "It's your duty."

Near the guns lay the cartridge pouches. Jonathan removed one cartridge.

Carefully, his fingers trembling, he went through the loading steps. This time, he did it right. The tearing of the cartridge. The pouring in of the powder. Wadding the ball. Stuffing it into the muzzle. Setting the firing grains in the pan . . . until it was all set.

Moving as quietly as he could, he went to the door and opened it. Gun in hand, he went out onto the porch and looked back in. He knew he would have but one shot, one shot and then he would run.

One shot.

Taking a deep breath, he drew back the flintlock and lifted the gun, then positioned himself in the doorway, one foot in, one foot out. His body began to tremble as he aimed the gun directly at the old soldier. He swallowed hard. He closed his eyes.

For a moment he saw and heard the fighting as it had been on the road. He opened his eyes and looked at the old soldier. His teeth clenched. He could feel tears on his face.

"Do it!"

He tried to pull the trigger. His fingers would not move. He could not shoot.

Jonathan slowly let the weight of the gun carry the muzzle down.

Swept by shame, he crept back into the house

and, afraid he'd be found out, quietly unloaded the gun and put it back where it had been. All the while he kept wiping tears from his face with his fingers. Then, on unsteady legs, he went outside, threw himself on the ground and looked up at the sky.

9:00

The crisp night air had cut away the mist. Overhead, stars had spread into a fancy, motelike glitter. Jonathan inhaled deeply, filling his chest with bright, biting air.

As he lay there, he saw himself as he had been that morning, listening to the tavern bell. The bell! He could feel himself—see himself—so eager to go to battle, to be a hero, to destroy the enemy. It seemed such a long time ago!

Despair choked him. Why, he asked himself, had he done so little? What was the matter with him? Why hadn't he been able to act?

Groping, he sought some way out, something to *do* that might redeem him.

It was then that he remembered the Corporal. He *had* seen him on the road. He was convinced of that. Perhaps he was close by, after all, looking for him. If he was, maybe he could find him.

Jonathan sat up.

He would tell the Corporal where the Hessians were. The Corporal would act for him.

9:15

Jonathan crept back into the house. After the cool outside air, the room was hot and smoky. The old soldier was now sprawled on the floor, fast asleep. The other soldiers had not moved.

The fire, though much lower, still gave Jonathan enough light to see by. By the table he studied the sleeping boy. He realized he could not leave him.

Jonathan went to the door, pulled it open, and returned to the table.

On hands and knees he drew the boy's sleeping box out, making a scratching sound. The young soldier shifted. Jonathan froze. When he was certain he was safe, he slipped his arms beneath the boy and gathered him up. The boy partially opened his eyes, only to close them again when he saw that it was Jonathan.

Jonathan wrapped his arms around him and pressed him to his shoulder. The boy seemed heavier than before.

At the door Jonathan stopped and looked about, sensing he had forgotten something. His gun. For a moment he considered taking it, but he knew he wouldn't be able to carry both the boy and the gun. Besides, it was too wet to be used. He turned and walked out the door, pulling it closed behind him.

9:30

Grateful for the moonlight, Jonathan walked a short distance from the house, holding the boy as best he could. His feet made hardly a sound. He had only the vaguest sense that he was crossing the field in the right direction. More than once he stopped, trying to find the direction from which he had come earlier in the day.

That was his only plan—to find the road. Once he found it, he would walk north. Sooner or later he was certain he would come to a place he'd recognize. From there he would somehow find the Corporal.

He shifted the boy on his shoulder. Unlike the first, brief time he had carried him, this time the boy did not hold on. Jonathan knew he would not be able to carry him for all the miles he needed to go. But he had to go much farther before he could take a rest.

He looked back. The soft glow of the paper window in the house was nothing more than a spot of gold.

Once more he adjusted his grip on the boy, then he continued to move across the dark field.

9:45

Jonathan bumped against the wooden fence. It took him by surprise, but he felt great relief. The first part of his escape was done. He was safely away and they hadn't noticed that he and the boy were gone.

It was difficult to get over the fence. With the boy in his arms he could not climb it. He had to lift him, put him over the rails, then lay him on the ground. It strained his arms, but he did it. The boy didn't wake.

Then Jonathan climbed over. On the other side he gathered the boy up again, placing him as high on his shoulder as he could. The boy stirred once, opened his eyes, and made a slight sound. Then, pressing against Jonathan's neck, he closed his eyes again.

IO:IO

Which way? Jonathan asked himself. On all sides he could see only the dark, slender silhouettes of trees, as if he were in a vast cage. The road, he knew, was not far off. But which way, and how close?

He turned around in a full circle, but knew no better than before. If anything, he was more confused.

He paused, then lifted the boy, who kept slipping, and forced himself to move, knowing he had to go somewhere, anywhere now, no matter what, or where.

10:15

As Jonathan moved among the trees, the darkness swallowed him. He wondered at its many shades, the many shapes of black that came before his eyes.

A high and fragmentary moon came and went elusively. All about, the forest spoke, sometimes sounds of animals, sometimes the white whirr of insect wings, sometimes only the trees shifting gently.

His eyes sought the road. More than once he staggered, but he did not fall. Several times he put the boy down to rest. Then he rose and, gathering him up, pushed on.

He felt as if he were going nowhere. The more he went, the more it seemed the same. Over and over again he asked himself: Where am I going? Is this the right way?

It was an hour before he saw a light.

11:20

At first he wasn't sure what it was. It seemed so small and flared only once, after which he lost sight of it. Still, it was enough to make him stop and wait. Putting the boy down, he stared at the place where he thought the light had been.

It did not return.

Just when he had decided it was only his imagination, the light flickered again. This time he was certain it was real.

He picked the boy up again. Holding him tightly though his arms ached, he began to move cautiously toward the light.

11:25

He could see the fire, and he heard low, muffled voices. Nervously, he waited. The boy by his shoulder stirred and made a sound. Jonathan put a hand to his mouth and the boy became quiet again. Jonathan gazed at the light and listened.

He knew they could be the other Hessians. "Americans," he prayed, "make them Americans."

Still more cautiously, he moved forward, trying to feel his way without making any sound, trying to see through the dark. As he drew closer, he could make out at least six forms hunched around the fire.

He crept forward. Soon he began to hear hushed words, and he strained to catch the language. German . . . or English?

"Halt!"

A form loomed up. Jonathan spun around, wanting only to flee. But when he turned, another person stood to block his way. That man was facing the fire. It was the Corporal.

11:35

Eight excited men circled Jonathan. Some held firebrands, some muskets. They gaped at him, pushed at him, touched him.

"What are you doing here?" the Corporal demanded. "What's your name? Where're you from?"

"He was with us at the tavern," cried one of the men. "He's the missing one! The one that ran. The one those Hessians were after!"

The Corporal snatched a burning stick from one of the men and brought it close. Jonathan felt the heat on his face. For a moment the Corporal stared at him, his own face masklike. Then he pulled back the flame.

"Where were you?" he said sharply.

Jonathan, exhausted, tongue-tied, took a quick look about the group of faces. They were all from the morning's fighting. Two of the men were bandaged. Jonathan held the boy tighter.

"I asked you where you were," the Corporal repeated harshly.

"Up the road," began Jonathan, struggling against his rising tears. "And when the fighting happened . . . when we were retreating . . . I . . . I ran. . . . Three of the Hessians caught me . . . made me prisoner. . . . Only"—he fumbled for words—"I . . . escaped."

"Who's that?" the Corporal wanted to know, pointing to the boy, whom Jonathan was still holding. "Where does he come from?"

Jonathan felt as if the question was an accusation.

"They took me to a place," he said. "A . . . house." He was finding it difficult to explain. "And he was there. I've been carrying him for a while. I . . . I have to put him down. I'm hungry."

The men, muttering words of encouragement, stepped away, allowing Jonathan to walk between them toward the fire. There, Jonathan carefully eased the boy down. The boy awoke with a start. Frightened, he stared at all the peering faces, refusing to let go of Jonathan. To keep him calm, Jonathan sat down at his side, aware mostly of his own great weariness.

Once again the men, curious, pressed close.

"Here you go," said one of them, reaching out a hand and offering him johnnycake. Jonathan gratefully took it, broke off a piece for the boy, then greedily devoured his own portion.

The Corporal squatted directly in front of Jonathan. "Those three soldiers," he said with barely surpressed urgency, "I need to know where you were with them."

Jonathan, not wanting to talk, thankful to be among friends, but knowing he must answer, tried to push away his fatigue. He looked up at the Corporal. "Back there some," he said.

"How far?"

Jonathan shook his head. "Not sure. I've been walking a time. I didn't know what they were going to do to me. At first, I thought they'd kill me. They kept me on a rope. I couldn't get away. Not till they fell asleep. They don't speak any English. They don't. Not one word. . . . I couldn't understand what they were saying. Nothing. I had to guess. It sounded bad." He took a deep breath, glancing around the circle to gauge the reaction. The men seemed concerned, kindly. His eyes came back to the Corporal.

Taking a breath, he continued. "I was sure I saw you on the road before," he said, "in all that fog. Didn't you see me? I was right there with them. On the rope so I couldn't get away. I couldn't . . ." He felt like he wanted to cry again and didn't know why. "I wanted to call out to you."

The Corporal's face was blank. Jonathan couldn't tell what he was thinking.

"I did see you," the Corporal said slowly. "But I was alone. There was nothing I could do. Go on. Tell the rest."

Jonathan closed his eyes and shook his head to clear his mind. "We went farther after that," he continued, "till we found the house. It was a cow needing to be milked that led us there. I milked her. They were . . . trusting me by then," he confessed. "Worst fog I ever did see. You couldn't tell which way to go. . . . Later on they tied me up again. I slipped the knot." He looked up, grateful for the rapt attention the men were giving him. He studied the Corporal's face again. It had changed. There was a look of suspicion.

"That house," said the Corporal carefully, "is that where you found the boy?"

Jonathan nodded.

"Anyone else there?"

Jonathan had begun to doze off. He jerked free of the drowsiness. "What?"

"I asked you: Was anyone else there?"

Jonathan looked about. Something had happened. He didn't understand what. Was it something he had said? The Corporal's voice had grown hard again, the questions more urgent. The man's stare made him uncomfortable.

"Anyone else?" the Corporal repeated.

Jonathan gazed at him, slightly nodding his head. "Who?"

"His parents," Jonathan said, indicating the boy. "I think it was them. Dead. Both of them. Killed. I found them out by a field. They had been just left there . . . like that."

The men murmured.

"It was . . . I think it was . . . I mean, I thought it was the Hessians who had killed them," Jonathan went on to say. "They acted strange, not like they cared at all . . . not surprised—as if they knew all about it. One of them, a young one, friendly, a bit, he said a prayer. Sounded like it. Maybe it wasn't. I couldn't tell." Now that he spoke about it, what he thought had happened no longer seemed so clear in his mind. He nodded toward the boy.

"I kept asking him about what happened. Lots of times. But he wouldn't say. Not a word. Anyway . . . I buried them. Thought it was right. . . ." Jonathan looked up and around. They were all staring at him. No one said a word. Some shifted uneasily.

"What happened?" asked Jonathan after a moment. "What happened when we were fighting?" He lowered his voice. "They licked us right bad, didn't they?"

"Nothing like," replied one of the men quickly. "More them than us got beat. Nope. Not us."

"Them!" cried Jonathan. He looked to the Corporal for confirmation. "Didn't they beat us?"

"We held them off," said the Corporal. "Held them enough so they didn't want any more. They went back."

"And faster than they came," threw in one of the men.

"Saving for those three that went after you," added another. "Must have thought they'd won and wanted to catch themselves a prize."

For a moment Jonathan felt the swell of pride. "Think so?" he said hopefully.

"Sure thing. Trade you in for a general," said one of the men.

Jonathan felt his face burn.

"We've been looking for them ever since they took after you," said another.

"Were you looking for me too?" asked Jonathan.

"Sure. Think we'd leave you, do you? Not us."

"I didn't know," said Jonathan, comforted by the words. "I was sure we got beat," he said.

"Not us. Them who turned scared and ran— wouldn't be us, would it?"

Guilt returned. "I ran," Jonathan said in a small voice.

"Don't you worry," said one of the men. "You're here. Don't you worry."

The Corporal, still squatting before him, reached out and shook his shoulder to get his attention. "Those three soldiers," he asked, "where are they now?"

"At the house," said Jonathan, trying to bring his thoughts and feelings together.

"By jingo, we can get them now," cried one of the men. "How far was that?" he asked.

"I don't know," replied Jonathan. "It was all so dark when I left. It's down the road some. That's all I know. I don't know any more." He wanted to stop, to sleep and go no farther.

But the questions only came faster than before.

"They know we're looking for them? They expecting us to show up?" Jonathan couldn't answer. He felt dizzy.

The Corporal put out a hand and cupped Jonathan's chin, turning his head so he would get all of his attention. "Did they post a guard?" he asked.

"No," Jonathan answered.

"We can get them then, easy," insisted someone. "He can lead us. Nothing to it."

"When you left them," continued the Corporal, paying no attention to anyone else, "what were they doing?"

"Sleeping," said Jonathan. Suddenly, he remembered—"I tried to kill them," he said, his voice faltering. "I really did. But I couldn't. I just . . . couldn't." Jonathan glanced at the boy, whose eyes were on the Corporal. He was trembling, and Jonathan wondered why.

"What happened to your gun?" the Corporal asked.

"I couldn't carry it and him," said Jonathan, feeling embarrassed. "I just couldn't." He shook his head. "I thought they had us licked bad. I really did." He looked up at the men and then at the Corporal, whose eyes were still fixed on him. "You going to get them? The Hessians?"

"You lead us and we'll do it," called a man.

Jonathan shook his head. "I don't know if I can," he said. "I'm not sure of the way. Before, I just walked. Anyway, I'm awful tired."

The Corporal withdrew his hand. "Doesn't matter," he said, and stood up. "I know where they are."

"You do?" said Jonathan, surprised.

The Corporal nodded yes. Jonathan stared at him. Something wasn't right. A small curl of suspicion began to twist inside Jonathan's stomach. The boy was still staring up at the Corporal, his face now full of fear. Jonathan waited for someone to speak. When no one did, he said, "How come?"

"How come what?" returned the Corporal.

"How come you know where they are?" asked Jonathan with a shaking voice. "You said you didn't do anything when you saw us. Did you follow?"

The Corporal shifted about as if the answer hung somewhere in the air. He said nothing.

Jonathan's unease continued to grow. He was completely awake now, and he studied the faces of the men. The smiles of a few moments before were gone. The men were nervously waiting for the Corporal to speak.

"Did you follow?" repeated Jonathan, suddenly not sure he wanted the answer.

The Corporal moved his head sharply, raking his eyes along the faces of the men. Then he looked down and gazed at Jonathan. "I was there," he said.

"At that house?"

"Yes."

"When?"

"Before."

"What do you mean, 'before'?"

"Last night."

"I don't understand," said Jonathan, struggling against the monstrous idea that had formed in his mind.

11:50

In the silence that followed, Jonathan felt an intense, suffocating pressure in his chest. It was as if his heart and lungs had been compacted into a hard, round ball, making it difficult for him to breathe.

"They were Tories," said the Corporal at last, as much to the men who were gathered around as to Jonathan. "French Papists, for that matter. Didn't speak a word of English. Least that's what they claimed. Try talking to him in French," he said, indicating the boy. "He'll give you a reply, I'd guess."

"But his father knew enough English to go spying for the Hessians in Trenton. That's what he was, a spy. Our Committee of Public Safety discovered it. Gentlemen," he said, appealing to the group, "what do you do when you discover a deadly snake? You destroy it, don't you?"

No one said a word. The little fire danced. Beyond, the trees stirred.

"There was an older boy there too," continued the Corporal. "He got away. He must have reached the Hessian garrison and informed them. As I told you gentlemen this morning, it was probably he who brought the Hessians out today, seeking some sort of revenge." He turned to face the men squarely. "You all knew that. What was done was an act of war. An enemy in civilian dress is a spy. Spies, when found, are executed."

"But my Snyderville Committee friends did not wish to see things through," the Corporal continued. "It took others. Brave men. Yourselves." As if suddenly remembering Jonathan, he swung about to look at him. "Does that answer your question?" he asked.

"What's the difference?" cut in one of the men. "We can get those three Hessians now, while they're sleeping. Just three of them. We've got all of us, don't we? Easy."

Jonathan struggled to his feet, then bent hurriedly to pick up the boy.

"I want to go home," he was just able to whisper.

The Corporal looked him over. "We're going to finish this first," he said. "And you're going to help. You're needed."

April 4, 1778

12:30

While the Corporal and most of the other men began their preparations, the Frenchman sat near Jonathan. He had a bandage around his head that was stained with dark blood. Another man stood nearby and looked on.

"You feel poor, I think," said the Frenchman. He spoke only a little above a whisper.

"Don't take it so hard," said the other man. "You did all right."

"That Corporal," continued the Frenchman, "he is one who believes in the struggle with all his heart. He believes, truly. I do not take an opposition to him." He glanced up at the other man, who nodded his agreement. The Frenchman went on. "Yes, it is difficult. Hard, perhaps. Very much. But you must not take it badly to yourself, my young friend."

"Happens all the time," put in the other.

"Soldiers," said the Frenchman, "they will get killed or they will do the killing. That is what happens."

"He's saying the truth," said the man.

Jonathan nodded, but felt that he did not truly understand.

"No one's going to blame you," said the man. "Will they?" he said to the Frenchman.

The Frenchman shook his head no. Then he turned to the boy. *"Et toi, mon beau,"* he said. *"Ça va?"*

Startled, the boy looked up. His face cleared with unfolding relief. *"Oh, monsieur,"* he began, *"mes parents . . ."* His words came quickly, tumbling faster and faster, mixed increasingly with crying and great heaving sobs. Jonathan looked on, astonished.

"See?" said the man to Jonathan. "He talks plenty."

The Frenchman listened to the boy intently, nodding, shaking his head, occasionally reaching out and touching the boy's face, his hand, his arm. As the boy talked, the man who had been looking on yawned and turned away, but not before tapping

Jonathan on the head and saying, "Don't you worry none." Then he was gone.

The boy continued to talk to the Frenchman. As he did so, he kept moving closer until when he was done, he had his head in the man's lap. The Frenchman stroked his hair.

"Is that what happened?" asked Jonathan, his voice hushed. "Did the Corporal kill them?"

The Frenchman looked about before speaking.

"He and a few others," he said, speaking quietly. "This 'Committee.' But he was in charge, as he is here. There was some . . . meeting. And, I believe, words. . . . You understand, an argument. . . . I don't know. Perhaps that man who was just here . . ." He searched for him, but he was no longer in sight. "Well, I don't know, then. . . ." He made an empty gesture with his free hand. "Well, his brother is— one hopes—safe, and somewhere."

Jonathan slumped down, trying to piece it all together. Then, after a moment, he asked: "In the fighting on the hill, before, did any of our side get killed?"

"Well, yes, alas, one person," said the Frenchman. "And another hurt badly on the shoulder. As for myself . . ." He put his fingers to his head. "I am almost not here."

Jonathan looked around. By the light of the fire he could see the Corporal talking to some of the men. They were listening carefully. From time to time they looked over in his direction. He realized that the man who had gotten killed was his father's friend. And at once he remembered him in the battle, his falling to the ground, the blood upon his blouse. That in turn reminded him of the boy's parents. He had found them on the ground.

Whose side, he asked himself, was he on?

Then into his mind floated the hints made about the Corporal at the tavern, and during the march. "Do people trust him?" he asked the Frenchman.

"Who is that?"

"The Corporal."

The Frenchman sighed, swiveled around to look across the camp, then turned to consider Jonathan. He shook his head. "Perhaps you should ask them. It is not a matter of the liking. No.

"Young friend, this Corporal is a man that is known as—well, how to say, a man who—fights. Bravely. When the fighting happens, yes, of course, he is what one wants. To be sure. But when the fighting stops, well, no, perhaps that is something that is different. Then, perhaps, you hope that he . . . that he is not there. Do you understand me?"

"What will happen to the boy?" asked Jonathan.

"Do not worry," said the Frenchman. "I will take him to my house. I shall, perhaps, if possible, seek to find that brother of his, who is, after all, somewhere. But you see, I have to be careful. But we shall do the best we can. My wife and me. There is no fault in the boy. But you?" he said to Jonathan. "What will become of you?"

Jonathan looked at the man, then looked down. His hand rested on the ground. It was cold. He did not have an answer.

4:30

Jonathan woke with a start. He had tried to keep awake, but it had been impossible.

It was the Corporal who had woken him, bending over and shaking him gently. It took a moment for Jonathan to realize that he was being offered some more johnnycake.

Taking it, he ate slowly, uncomfortable under the eyes of the Corporal.

"You have had a bad time, haven't you?" said the Corporal.

Jonathan, hearing unexpected kindness in the voice, stopped eating and looked up, puzzled. By the firelight the man's face was deeply lined and looked terribly tired. Jonathan was reminded of the old soldier. The Corporal's green jacket, which had begun the day before in poor-enough condition, was now torn about the shoulder, exposing tattered lining. He no longer wore a hat. Jonathan wondered if he was as poor a man as he appeared.

"How old are you?" asked the Corporal.

"Thirteen."

"Listen to me," he said.

Jonathan looked up into the man's face. He saw sadness there.

"You did very well," said the man.

"Did I?"

"The best you could. Want some more?" He offered more johnnycake.

Jonathan shook his head.

"Sure?"

"Yes."

"You ready to go?"

Jonathan dropped his gaze to the ground.

"Are you?"

Jonathan, without looking up, shook his head. He whispered: "I don't want to."

"You must."

"Why?"

"Soldiers do what they're told to do," said the Corporal. His voice was almost soothing. "And you're a soldier. You're needed."

"What for?"

"You'll see." The Corporal held out his hand. After a moment's hesitation, Jonathan took it, surprised at its hardness. He stood up and looked about. Most of the men were gathered in a group.

"Where's the boy?" asked Jonathan, suddenly feeling the absence of the child, who was no longer by his side.

"The Frenchman took care of him. They're gone."

"I want to go too."

The Corporal shook his head.

"Please." Jonathan wanted to look at the Corporal but found he could not. He looked instead into the near distance, at the knot of men. One of them had a torch. It was the one who had spoken with him and the Frenchman before he slept. All the others had muskets. They were waiting.

The Corporal reached out, took Jonathan's arm, and eased him forward. "It's time to see this through," he said in a lifeless tone.

5:00

The Corporal carried a musket in his right hand while his left rested on Jonathan's shoulder. His touch was light, and there were moments when Jonathan wasn't even sure if it was there. Still, he sensed that if at any moment he should try to flee, the hand would instantly hold him fast.

Right behind them came the man with the torch. It was the only light they carried, and its flame was small, just enough for them to find their way. Jonathan felt as if he was walking deep into a cave.

They went quietly and quickly, the Corporal setting a steady pace. The only sounds were their muffled steps, crackling twigs, rustling leaves.

They reached the road. Overhead, the moon was bright. In the open sky there were few stars.

The Corporal insisted that they move with haste lest the Hessians be gone. He wanted to arrive just at dawn. "But make sure your guns are ready now," he commanded.

It was done.

"We going to hold them for ransom or exchange?" asked one of the men as they went.

"We'll see," the Corporal replied.

"Too bad none of us speak German," said another.

"What for?" came the retort. "Nothing to talk about."

"No more chatter," said the Corporal sharply. "And stay together."

He took the lead, with Jonathan held close.

5:30

The Corporal held up his hand and stopped. The men crowded around.

"It's in there," said the Corporal, speaking softly.

"You sure?"

"No question."

"How far?"

"A few hundred yards along the path and we'll reach their fields. No more than that."

"What's it like there?"

For the first time Jonathan felt the hand on his shoulder tighten. "Tell him," the Corporal said.

"It's . . . it's a small house," Jonathan stammered.

"Louder."

"A small house."

"Back door?"

Jonathan hesitated.

"Tell them," the Corporal said.

"No," said Jonathan.

"And they're just sleeping in there?"

"Yes, sir."

"Ducks in a pond."

The Corporal gave Jonathan a slight push.

"This way," he said.

5:35

The path they followed led them easily through the woods, taking them directly to the fence. There they stopped and looked across the field. The house stood in silhouette, small but distinct. The paper window let out a faint orange glow.

"There it be," said someone.

"Sweet and easy."

"Quiet!" hissed the Corporal.

They stood silently, staring across the empty field. An owl called twice. Jonathan could hear the breathing of the men, the slight, nervous shifting of their feet. He tried to see their faces. He wondered how they felt. Was he, he wondered, the only one who didn't want to be there?

He looked at the sky. A faint gray haze hung in the east.

"We only need to cover the front door," said the Corporal softly. "The boy says there's no other way out. That's my memory too. What we'll do is this: move across the field in a line. Keep your muskets ready, aiming at that door. They just might be up and ready to fight."

"Can't we just jump in?"

"Too risky. For all I know they're getting ready. We don't know what we'll find. The boy can go right to the door, open it, and see what they're doing." He spoke as if Jonathan was not standing there. "So if they're up," he continued, "they won't suspect anything."

"Tied him up, didn't they?" put in someone.

"Yeah. Maybe they've already seen he's gone."

"They're liable to suspect something."

"He said they got to trusting him," said the Corporal. "Didn't you?" he asked Jonathan.

All eyes turned to Jonathan.

"Didn't you?" the Corporal repeated.

Jonathan, realizing what he was being asked to do, nodded numbly.

"Right," said the Corporal. "Now, just walk easy. If something happens, get out of the way. If nothing, you can get right to the door and open it. See what you can see. But you don't have to go farther. Just poke your head inside and find out if they're sleeping or not. Then get out of the way, fast."

"*Fast,*" agreed an echoing voice.

"Is that clear?" the Corporal asked Jonathan.

Jonathan closed his eyes. He felt ill.

"Is it?"

He nodded.

"Now," said the Corporal briskly, "go on. Get to it. And be careful, you hear?"

5:38

Jonathan stood before the fence, desperately wanting not to go.

"Didn't you hear me?" said the Corporal. "Now."

"Go on, boy," encouraged another. "It'll be all right. Nothing's going to happen to you."

"Move," said the Corporal, his voice tightening.

Slowly, Jonathan climbed the fence and dropped to the other side. It was then that the Corporal reached across the top rail and for a moment held Jonathan's arm.

"Do exactly what I told you to do," he said, "and you'll be safe."

Jonathan remained where he was, unmoving.

"You ran before," said the Corporal to Jonathan. "Didn't you?"

Jonathan nodded.

The Corporal's voice was low. "Now all you have to do is let us know if they're sleeping or not. *That's all.*"

Jonathan was afraid to look up.

"Didn't you hear him, boy?" called one of the men.

"They didn't hurt me," said Jonathan, his voice small. "They didn't—"

"You wanted to come, didn't you? Wanted to fight?" said the Corporal. "Answer me!"

"Yes, sir."

"Be all right" came an encouraging voice. "We'll be watching."

Still Jonathan stood.

Reaching across the fence again, the Corporal turned Jonathan so hard that the boy stumbled. All the same, he looked back. The men were watching him. The Corporal pointed toward the house. Jonathan remained where he was. "Please," he said, appealing to the men. He knew he had tears on his face.

The Corporal cocked the flintlock of his gun. A trickle of horror, like a finger sliding up his spine, came to Jonathan.

"Do it," said the Corporal, *"now."*

Slowly, Jonathan turned and began to walk toward the house.

5:45

When Jonathan had covered half the distance to the house, he stopped and looked back. The Americans were lined behind the fence, standing in a dark row like cemetery stones against the blue-gray sky. Their muskets were black staffs. Their eyes, possumlike, alone contained some faint light.

He heard the cow shifting her weight by the shed. Again he looked at the Americans. The Corporal raised a hand and urged him on.

Turning, Jonathan moved again toward the house.

He stepped up on the porch. It gave a slight creak. At the door he put a hand to the latch. Again he looked back, paused, then pushed. The door swung open. He could see nothing. He took one more look behind him, then he walked inside.

5:50

The fire in the hearth was nothing more than a glow. The room smelled of burned wood. All he could hear was the breathing of the soldiers. They were fast asleep, exactly as he had left them: the young one on the bed, the tall one on the floor before the hearth, the old one in his corner, the rope still attached to his ankle.

Nothing had changed. They had not noticed he had gone.

Jonathan knew exactly what he was supposed to do next; turn around and return to the Corporal, tell him that the Hessians were still asleep.

He gazed about the room again, sighed, then turned and moved toward the door. The old soldier murmured in his sleep. It was enough to make Jonathan stop and swing about once more. He stared at the sleeping man. His head was throbbing, the pain inside unbearable.

Whose side was he on?

Slowly, he reached out and lightly touched the door. It swung shut, leaving him inside.

For a moment he just stood there, trying to understand what he had done.

Then, with a quick move, he came to life. He leaned against the door and latched it. Hurriedly, he went to where the young soldier slept. Crouching down, he shook him.

Groaning slightly, partly opening his eyes, the young soldier awoke for a moment, then dropped back to sleep.

Jonathan shook his arm again, harder this time. Once more the Hessian opened his eyes, finally managing to focus on Jonathan. With an effort he pushed himself up on his elbow.

"Was gibt's?" he said, his voice crusted with sleep.

"Soldiers," said Jonathan in a strained whisper. "Americans . . . soldiers . . . *Soldat!*" he said, remembering the word the young soldier had taught him. *"Soldat,"* he repeated, pointing toward the door.

"They're right outside," said Jonathan. Again he pointed. "They'll kill you if you don't give up. Soldiers. *Soldat!*"

With sudden comprehension, the young soldier

sat up, knocking Jonathan away so hard the boy fell backward.

The Hessian looked about the room, his eyes wide. Then he jumped to his feet, moved to the door, and tried to open it. He fumbled with the latch, released it, opened the door, looked out, only to slam it shut.

"Auf! Auf!" he cried, moving from one soldier to the other. *"Angriff! Angriff!"*

The two pushed themselves up and stared stupidly at him.

"Die Amerikaner! Sie sind draussen!" the young soldier shouted.

As if to echo what he said, a volley of shots smashed up against the wood house like a host of hammers.

The two other Hessians leaped to their feet. Casting aside furniture that lay in their paths, they rushed for their guns.

Jonathan, crouching on the floor to one side, looked on in terror.

A second round of shots slammed against the house. One ball split the paper window and struck against the hearth with a hard, shattering crack. A chunk of stone fell to the floor.

"Surrender!" came a voice from outside. It was the Corporal's voice. "You're surrounded. Give yourselves up. Your lives will be spared."

The Hessians, completely disheveled, unbuttoned, bootless, listened intently. They stood in the middle of the room, guns in their hands, with looks of utter stupefaction on their faces.

"Surrender or be killed!" came the Corporal's voice again.

Jonathan listened, horrified. The Corporal knew the Hessians understood no English—Jonathan had *told* him.

It was the old soldier who finally reacted. Leaping for his knapsack, he ripped out his cartridge case and powder, loaded his gun, and thrust on his bayonet. The rope—the rope to which Jonathan had been tied—remained tied to his ankle and flayed about like a writhing snake.

The other Hessians frantically prepared their guns. As they did, the old soldier edged forward, the rope trailing, and yanked open the door, then leaped to one side.

Rapidly, he spoke to the others, a flood of words to which the other two blankly nodded. While he spoke, the old soldier kept checking his gun, making sure it was ready.

Jonathan, realizing that they were going to attempt to fight their way out, began to shout: "They'll kill you if you try. They will. Just give up. Give up!"

At the sound of his voice, the old soldier spun about, took two long steps across the room, and made a grab for Jonathan. Jonathan tried to dodge away, scrambling toward the door on his hands and knees. The Hessian snatched at him, missed, grabbed again. Catching Jonathan's foot, he dragged him back and whipped him upright. With an iron grip his arm instantly went around Jonathan's neck as he yanked him up against his body like a shield.

Jonathan, gasping for breath, writhed and clawed at the Hessian's arm, while the old soldier shouted orders to his companions.

Twisting wildly, attempting to turn and kick, even to bite the soldier's arm, Jonathan kept trying to free himself. In response, the old soldier brought his knee sharply up against the small of his back. The pain was intense, and his struggle faltered. The old soldier held him closer yet.

The young soldier cried out: *"Lass ihn los! Lass ihn los!"*

The old soldier barked an answer. The young one stood still, his chest heaving, rubbing a hand over his sweaty forehead, through his hair, around his mouth. He nodded.

Again the old soldier spoke sharply.

Jonathan, realizing he could not free himself, called out, "Don't do it. Give up. They'll kill you!"

The old soldier responded by tightening his grip around his neck, making it hard for him to breathe.

"*Fertig?*" whispered the old soldier to the others. They nodded.

The old soldier, one arm around the boy, the other hand gripping his gun, inched toward the door. The two others pressed close behind.

They reached the doorway. Jonathan could see out. Fifty feet in front of the house the Americans were standing in a semicircle, guns to their shoulders, aiming at the doorway.

"*Los!*" grunted the old soldier and stepped into the doorway. Jonathan twitched spasmodically. The grip around his neck tightened. He was choking.

In a knot of tangled arms, legs, and muskets, the four of them wedged into the doorframe. Searching for his footing, Jonathan looked at the Americans—their guns ready. The Hessian pressed him from behind. They edged out to the porch and stood on the top step.

In a last, desperate effort, Jonathan twisted violently, butting his head into the old soldier's chest. For an instant the Hessian lost his grip. Jonathan wildly struck out with his arms. The soldier teetered at the top of the porch and released Jonathan. Instantly, Jonathan pulled away and, dropping low, dove back into the house.

The Hessians, now unshielded and completely exposed, stood frozen, then seemed to tumble forward. Jonathan spun about in the doorway just as the rope, still attached to the old Hessian's ankle, whipped by. Impulsively, Jonathan reached out and tried to hold it. He held it for less than a second. The burn of its passing seared his hand.

The old Hessian tripped, and so close was he to the other two, so entangled, that they too fell.

There was a roar of shots.

And then—silence.

6:10

Jonathan stared out. The morning had turned milk white. The three Hessians were upon the ground, their bodies twisted, their torn uniforms filthy with earth and blood. The Corporal and the other men gathered around in a semicircle, gazing at the dead.

Jonathan watched the Americans turn and, guns in their hands or on their shoulders, start to walk slowly back across the field. As he watched, they grew faint, shrouded in the rising morning mist. No one looked back, or spoke, or paused. They just left.

6:13

Only the Corporal remained. He kept looking at the fallen men. Slowly, he bent down and gently closed their eyes. Then he gathered up their guns. When he stood, he became aware that Jonathan had come from the house and was close by. They looked at one another.

"You tried to save them, didn't you?" said the Corporal.

"Yes."

"They would have killed you."

"They didn't."

The Corporal looked beyond Jonathan to the house, then to the line of retreating men, then to the rising sun. He seemed to speak to the air. "They killed one of ours yesterday. And you don't know how many others before. At Long Island, they bayoneted the wounded. They were soldiers. So am I. So are you. You were lucky, that's all. There's nothing more to it."

Jonathan stared at him. The Corporal attempted to return the look. Suddenly, he turned away and said: "Go get your gun. It doesn't belong to you. It needs returning."

Heavily, Jonathan turned and went back inside the house. It took time for him to find his gun, buried as it was beneath the rubble of the room.

Slowly, he pulled it clear and grasped it in his hands. He looked down at it. Then, lifting it, holding it by the barrel, he swung it over his head. With the surging strength of his exploding rage, he brought it down against the stone hearth. The shock shot through his bones. The gun almost fell from his grasp. But now his rage had seized him completely, pouring through him. Gripping the gun even tighter, he began pounding it against the stones, again and again and again.

The gun stock splintered. The metal bent and burst. Pieces flew in all directions. He fell to his knees sobbing.

Jonathan felt a hand tighten on his shoulder. "Come," said the Corporal. "It's time to go."

6:40

They walked in silence. Even when they caught up with the other men, no one spoke.

Jonathan stayed in the rear. No one walked close to him or spoke to him. He wasn't bothered. It was better that way. All he wanted to do was move.

When they reached the camp, a wounded man who had remained there asked what had happened.

"They tried to get away," said one of the men. "Tried to fight when we offered surrender."

"Fools!"

Jonathan looked about for the boy and the Frenchman, only to remember that they had long gone.

The men gathered up their things and headed north, leaving the camp behind.

As they walked, they moved in small groups of twos and threes. Jonathan went alone. At one point the Corporal came and attempted to march by his side.

Instantly, Jonathan stopped.

The Corporal stopped too.

"Leave me alone," said Jonathan.

The Corporal, momentarily flustered, started to say something, stopped, and walked away. And it was only then that Jonathan wondered what had happened to his horse. But after that Jonathan was left to himself.

9:30

By the time Jonathan reached the tavern, only four of the men remained. The rest had slipped away. When Jonathan realized where they'd come to, he stopped. Automatically he looked for the Corporal. But the Corporal too had gone.

The tavern keeper, grinning broadly, ran out to meet them, shaking hands all around. "Beat them, did you!" he cried. "A famous victory, gentlemen. A drink to celebrate our victory."

Only one of the men accepted.

After a few moments the tavern keeper realized that Jonathan was there. "Ah, you," he said. "Your father came a-looking for you. Had permission, did you? You're a sly boots, you are. He would have gone right after you if he wasn't dragging that leg of his. And him sick with your going. You'll be wanting to go home right quick, you will."

Jonathan said nothing and started to move. Then the innkeeper remembered.

"Hey," he called. "Where's my gun?"

Jonathan stopped and turned. "It's gone."

"Gone? What happened to it? You gave me your word, boy."

Jonathan, not wanting to explain, simply walked away.

"The honor of your word," cried the tavern keeper after him. "I'll be after your pa!"

10:30

Jonathan reached home.

When he stepped into the clearing before their house, no one was about. The only thing moving was smoke rising from the chimney. For a moment he studied the doorway, preparing himself to go in.

But as he stood there a vague, soft chopping

sound came. He listened. It was the sound of a hoe striking against the earth. It was as if a clock had begun to tick again.

Turning, Jonathan walked to the field, moving amidst the trees, his steps keeping pace with the sound. It filled him, pushing away the pain.

Briefly he stopped, feeling as though he was seeing a mirage; it was himself he seemed to see, himself as he had been the day before, rushing headlong from the field.

He moved on, slower now, stepping from the woods to the edge of the field. There was his father, working the ground. Jonathan watched him silently, watching the slow, limping shuffle and stride of the weakened leg.

Something made his father stop and look around, until his eyes rested on Jonathan. For a moment the two merely looked at one another, as if each needed to be sure the other was truly there.

Then, like a flame rekindled, Jonathan saw the fear in his father's eyes.

"Were you . . . hurt?" his father stammered.

Jonathan, unable to talk, shook his head. No.

His father let out a long breath. "Praise God," he said. "I am glad, so glad, boy." And he smiled.

And there, then, at last, Jonathan understood that his father's fear had not been for himself. No, it was for Jonathan, that *he* might be spared.

And suddenly, Jonathan understood more. Understood the most important thing—that he had indeed been spared.

Oh, how glad he was to be there.

And alive.

Oh, alive.

THE GERMAN TRANSLATED

3:47

Siehst du was?
Do you see anything?

3:50

Er erschiesst uns, wenn wir nicht vorsichtig sind.
He'll shoot us if we're not careful.
*Weg von hier. Es ist blöd und gefährlich. Wir finden
    ihn nie.*
Let's get out of here. It is stupid and dangerous.
    We'll never find him.
Noch ein Paar Minuten.
A couple more minutes.
Ich hab's satt.
I'm sick of it.
Mein Gott! Vor unseren Augen!
My God! Right before our eyes!

Es ist nur ein Junge.

It's only a boy.

Komm hierher!

Come here.

Idiot! Die verstehen nie. Komm hierher, Junge!

Idiot! They never understand anything. Come here, boy.

Das ist besser.

That's better.

Halt!

Stop!

Wir sprechen kein Englisch. Warum sprichst du kein Deutsch?

We don't speak any English. Why don't you speak any German?

Dreh dich um!

Turn around.

Los, er macht vor Angst in die Hosen.

Come on, he's so scared he's making in his pants.

Steh auf! Es tut dir keiner was.

Get up. No one's going to do anything to you.

4:01

Warte!

Wait.

Es ist ein schönes Land.

It's a beautiful country.

Los, geh!
Go on, move.

5:00

Steh auf!
Get up.

5:15

Wir haben uns verirrt.
We're lost.
*Vielleicht sind wir geschlagen. Vielleicht sind wir die
    einzigen am Leben!*
Maybe we were beaten. Maybe we're the only ones
    left alive!
Gott helf uns!
God help us!

5:20

O Gott!
Oh God!
Es ist nichts.
There's nothing.
Doch, da war was!
There *was* something!

155

5:40

Los! Mach die Tür auf!
Go on. Open the door.
Los!
Go on!
Noch einmal!
Again!
Was war das?
What was that?
Melken. Wir können dann die Milch trinken.
Milking. Then we can drink the milk.

5:50

Los, geh!
Go on, move!
Fertig?
Finished?

6:35

Mein Gott!
My God!
Woher kommt denn der?
Where did *he* come from?
Was sagt er?
What's he saying?

6:45

Nun komm!
Come on!
Komm!
Come!

7:40

Das genügt.
That'll have to do.
Halt ihn fest.
Hold him tight.
Los, beeil dich!
Come on, hurry up!

5:50

Was gibt's?
What's going on?
Auf! Auf! Angriff! Angriff!
Get up! Get up! Attack! Attack!
Die Amerikaner! Sie sind draussen!
The Americans! They're outside!
Lass ihn los! Lass ihn los!
Let him go! Let him go!
Fertig?
Ready?
Los!
Move!

Die suxer